Cowboy Dreaming Alone

Coming Home to North Dakota Book Five

Jessie Gussman

Acknowledgments

Cover art by Julia Gussman
   Editing by Heather Hayden
   Narration by Jay Dyess
   Author Services by CE Author Assistant

Listen to a FREE professionally performed and produced audiobook version of this title on Youtube. Search for "Say With Jay" to browse all available FREE Dyess/Gussman audiobooks.

Contents

Chapter 1

Overlooking small things.
- Paula Hurdle from Mississippi

"That's gorgeous! Even better than I had pictured!" Sadie exclaimed as she looked at the mailbox that Shasta Bingley had just handed her.

Shasta smiled, although she tried not to show her relief. Her last client had been a huge job, a wall mural that had taken her a month, and he still hadn't paid her.

She had been hoping that Sadie would like her work on the decorative mailbox, and she'd been hoping even harder that Sadie would pay her.

Today.

"I'm so glad you like it." Truly, that was the best part of her job, seeing the expressions on her clients' faces when they saw her work.

But expressions didn't pay the bills. She tried not to hold her breath as Sadie exclaimed over the intricate details of the flowers and the bird's nest and even the shiny blue robin eggs that were nestled in it.

"This mailbox is a work of art. I feel like I should mount this in my living room and not have it sitting out on my driveway." Sadie ran a gentle finger over an intricately painted daisy. "It's just breathtaking."

Sadie's appreciation was almost enough to make Shasta forget about the overdue rent, her empty cupboards, and her even more empty stomach.

She'd grown up in Nebraska and had met Sadie in college where they'd been roommates all four years. Sadie had talked so well about Sweet Water, North Dakota, that Shasta had vowed to move there as soon as she was able.

The thing she hadn't thought of, and now felt stupid about, was that in a small town, there were very few clients who would be interested in, or could afford, the kind of work she did.

Sadie loved her work, but Shasta had a hunch that Sadie had ordered the mailbox more out of pity than because she really wanted it.

Still, she wasn't too proud to take pity work right now. She needed everything she could get, and she needed to be paid for it, too.

"And these hummingbirds. They're so lifelike! You have definitely gotten better than you were even in college, and you amazed me then."

Shasta had painted everything she could get her hands on in college. She'd even gotten in trouble for painting on the walls of her dorm. But rather than fining her, the college had just made her stay and help the contractors repaint all the walls in the dorms during summer break.

It hadn't been too bad, because after she put in her required hours, the contractor had hired her, and she had a job the rest of the summer.

It wasn't the kind of painting she loved, but it was a job, first of all, and second, every day she got to make big, white canvases and paint them in her mind with all kinds of beautiful things.

"Don't you think so, Nolt?" Sadie said, looking behind Shasta.

Shasta had been lost in her head and hadn't been paying attention, so it surprised her when a man walked up beside her, leaning over, indulgence on his face until he actually started looking at the work, and his expression soon turned to sharp interest.

Nolt, Sadie's brother.

While she'd only seen him once, he had the same tall, broad-shouldered, confident look that she had admired from afar while in college. From afar because Nolt was twelve years older than his sister, Sadie. Twelve years older than herself, and in college, twelve years was a lifetime.

She'd never told Sadie that she'd secretly crushed on her oldest brother, partly because the idea was so preposterous, and also partly because Sadie had already confided in her that Nolt had fallen in love in high school, but his crush had chosen someone else, and he'd never gotten over it.

Sadie had said he was one of those who fall in love one time and only once in a lifetime kind of guys.

Regardless, she was definitely not in a position to be in a relationship anyway. She'd struggled since college to make a living with her art, usually having to have side jobs like waitressing that had nothing to do with how she truly wanted to make her living.

Here in Sweet Water, unless she worked on a ranch, or in a trucking company, or for the feed mill, there wasn't much else since the diner wasn't hiring.

"It's good," Nolt finally said, straightening up and glancing at her with an expression that Shasta could only term disinterest.

She didn't look at him long, though, because she had another coughing fit. She turned her head and put her arm over her mouth, coughing into her elbow.

The coughing had gotten worse since it started a couple of days ago, and she felt like she was going to cough up a lung.

If she were taking stock of her symptoms, she would say she felt feverish, but she couldn't afford to not work, and she couldn't afford to be sick, so she decided it was just a little warm in the office. At least that's what she told herself.

"That cough sounds serious," Sadie said with concern.

Shasta coughed for a couple more seconds before she cleared her throat and swallowed. "It's nothing."

She thought she heard Nolt snort but couldn't say for sure.

Regardless, Sadie lifted her brows and said, "You probably ought to get it checked out."

"I will," Shasta said, cringing a little inside, because the words were most likely not true. She couldn't afford to eat, let alone go to the doctor. She'd do it if she could, so maybe she got bonus points for it being true if it were possible.

Still, the lie didn't sit well, and she stared at the floor, knowing she should probably take her leave but staying for just a few more seconds, because she was really hoping Sadie would remember to pay her.

"Something like that must cost a fortune," Nolt said, causing Shasta to smile. He'd said it was good, like it was an elementary school art project.

Maybe he liked it after all.

"Oh! You almost let me forget to pay you." Sadie pulled out a drawer in her desk and took her purse out, pulling out her wallet and a checkbook.

Sadie almost groaned. It was Friday evening, and the banks were closed. Monday was the Fourth of July, and she wouldn't be able to cash that check until Tuesday.

At least she'd had the twenty dollars required to open an account in town. So she had a bank; she just couldn't use it until Tuesday.

Still, she smiled gratefully and thanked Sadie as she ripped the check out of the book and handed it over.

"This mailbox might be really good advertisement for you, as much as it kills me to think of it sitting outside along the road. People will see it, and it will definitely be a conversation starter." Sadie beamed, excited. "I'm sure it will earn you a lot of work and requests for not just mailboxes but a ton of different things. You can paint anything."

Shasta gave Sadie a grateful smile, even though she had to dis-agree. "You've always believed in me. Thank you." So many people hadn't. And a lot of people had been right, telling her that she would never make a living from her art and she should choose a major in college that would actually pay the bills and do art on the side.

It was reasonable advice, and she probably should have taken it, but she wanted to study art, and she went all in. Determined that if she put everything she had into it, it would have to work out.

Nope. That was wrong. Even if she put her heart and soul and everything she had, literally, into her art, it didn't mean it was going to work out.

It didn't even mean that she was going to eat.

"It's Friday evening," Nolt said quietly from beside her. She'd almost forgotten he was even there.

Shasta wasn't sure what to say. If Sadie didn't pay her cash, she wouldn't be eating until Tuesday. But not only did she hate to admit her desperate straits, she hated even worse admitting them in front of Nolt. Also, she didn't want to put anyone out. The mailbox had only been a couple hundred dollars, but who carried that kind of cash around?

Before she could figure out what she was going to say, which would most likely have been a polite refusal, Nolt was pulling his wallet out of his back pocket.

"How much was it?" he asked, and when Shasta looked up, he wasn't looking at her but at his sister.

Sadie rattled off the amount, and Nolt pulled the bills from his wallet.

He held his wallet in such a way that Shasta couldn't see what all was in it, even if she had been seriously looking, which she wasn't. She was just peeking out of the corner of her eye. But it wasn't like he was flashing his money or anything. That would have been ostentatious and a real turnoff. It wasn't like that at all. And she couldn't help feeling grateful for his consideration.

"I'm sorry, I never even thought."

"It's okay. Normally I would be protesting rather strongly right now," Shasta said as she pulled the check out of her pocket and handed it to Sadie who ripped it up. "But I just did a month-long project for a man in Nebraska where I lived, it was a huge wall mural, and he hasn't paid me for it."

"And moving is expensive." Nolt made that comment like it was the most natural thing in the world, although Shasta knew for a fact that the man had never lived anywhere but Sweet Water, North Dakota.

"It is. And I needed first and last months' rent on my place here in town, and it just wiped me out." Plus getting there, a couple nights of lodging as she looked for an apartment, and little odds and ends that cropped up. Including a flat tire along the interstate.

She literally had nothing, other than a place to lay her head. Actually, her apartment didn't even boast a bed or couch. Although she did have a kitchen chair that had been left there by the last occupant.

Nolt held out the cash, and she took it, murmuring a thank you, which triggered another coughing spell.

"You need Sadie to take you to the critical care center in Rockerton?" Nolt asked when she was finally done.

She shook her head, not wanting to say anything and trigger more. She was already embarrassed enough. Coughing, needing cash, and now obviously they assumed that she wasn't adult enough to take herself to the doctor if she needed to.

Which was true, but still.

"Are you sure?" Sadie asked, concern etched on her brow.

"Yes."

The room spun. Shasta tried to concentrate to keep from swaying and losing her balance. That last coughing fit had been the worst, and she wanted to go to her apartment and lie down. On the floor, but at least she had a towel she could use as a pillow.

At any rate, she needed to get out of here before she fell. She didn't want to bother these people anymore. They had already been more kind than she deserved.

Once she'd lain down for a bit, maybe she'd be able to get up and get some groceries. Now that she could afford it.

And some cough medicine.

Giving Sadie a hug and waving at Nolt who nodded his head, she hurried out as fast as she could, determined to get some rest before she worried about how she was going to earn money.

Lord. Please send work.

Chapter 2

Trust.
- Amanda Kuhse from Illinois

"We were hoping you would take this to the new girl in town...Shasta," Miss Charlene said, handing a box to Nolt.

When the ladies had called him to the church basement where the Piece Makers regularly met, Nolt had thought they needed him to fix something or give them a hand around one of their properties.

Maybe even give them a ride.

But he knew what this meant.

"I'll take it to the garage, and I'll have Sadie deliver it."

Miss Charlene froze with her mouth open, her blue hair waving gently as she glanced at the other ladies as though looking to them for help.

Nolt hid a grin as they looked at her with deer-in-the-headlight expressions, like they weren't sure how to handle him.

He took pity on them.

"Listen, I know what you did with my brother Silas and Gladys. And with a couple of my other brothers. People are on to you. Although, I think people appreciate what you're doing."

"I don't know what you're talking about," Miss Charlene said, still fighting to hold onto the cloak of being anonymous.

"I'm talking about you working to manipulate people's lives in order to get couples together. Playing Cupid." Nolt gave Miss Charlene an easy smile. "I appreciate it, actually. My brothers need to get married, and when you match people up in Sweet Water, they have a tendency to stay here. Our town is benefiting from young married couples choosing to raise their families here. I'm not complaining."

Miss Charlene put her hands on her hips, her lips flat and her expression annoyed. "Then why are you not cooperating? You need to deliver this quilt, and you need to do it yourself!"

"I appreciate it for other people, but I'm not available. Not interested. I'm not going along with it."

"You sure look like you're available to me," Miss Kathy said, looking pointedly at his bare left ring finger.

"I don't have any interest in being married. And especially not to the little girl in the apartment you're sending me to."

"She's a grown woman. She's out of high school and graduated from college. I have it on good authority from Patty's Diner," Miss Teresa said, always wanting to make sure everything was accurate.

"That makes her twelve years younger than me, because she was my baby sister's college roommate. Regardless of the age difference, although that's an issue, there's someone else, and I'm not interested."

"You're dating?" Miss Charlene said, her brows going up, showing her surprise.

"No."

Normally he didn't talk to the quilting ladies this much, but he figured that he'd be dodging their attempts to set him up with Shasta—and he didn't have any trouble remembering her name, he just acted like he did so they wouldn't jump on the fact that he knew it as proof that he was interested—unless he set the record straight. Which he just did.

"You're not married," Miss Vicki said, her voice thoughtful.

"No."

"Then you're available."

"No." He couldn't explain to them that he'd fallen in love once, and for him, he'd never fall in love again. Alana had been the only one, and she would always be the only one.

It still pinched a little to think about her choosing Jack over him. He hadn't tried to keep up with her after that.

But he thought about her a lot. Tried not to covet, and definitely tried not to wish things had turned out differently. In his experience, it was always better to look forward than back.

"There is no reason why you can't deliver the quilt." Miss Charlene crossed her arms over her chest and lifted a brow at him, like he was an errant child, instead of a six-foot-tall thirty-four-year-old adult.

"And there's no reason why Sadie can't do it either. They're great friends, and Sadie will be thrilled to go visit Shasta for a bit."

"Well, Sadie can't do it, because she's busy." Miss Charlene shrugged her shoulders and held her hands out, like she was going to take the box from him.

"What do you mean? She's not busy. She's at the trucking company office where she always is, and—"

"She just left," Miss Teresa said, holding up her phone. The screen showed some kind of text, although she was too far away from Nolt for him to be able to read it.

"She just left? She didn't have anywhere to go today." He didn't know that for sure, but usually when Sadie took off, he knew it. Marigold, their sister-in-law, took over for her... Sadie had a ski trip coming up, but she wouldn't be taking Miss Teresa shopping if she was on her trip.

"She did. She's on her way here to pick me up, because I have to go to the store."

"You do?" Nolt said, his eyes narrowing at Miss Teresa. "I suppose that need to go to the store just popped up, oh, I don't know, a minute and a half ago."

"It might have. Still, Sadie is busy."

"She can do it after she takes you to the store."

"We're going to the mall in Rockerton. We won't be back until tonight," Miss Teresa said, and Nolt had to hand it to her, she could think pretty fast on her feet.

Normally, he didn't go for the easy way. He was always looking for the best way, but in this instance, when he had four ladies working against him, the best thing to do seemed to be to capitulate and just take the quilt.

He moved the box a little away from Miss Charlene's outstretched hands. "I'll take it. But don't get your hopes up. Because what you guys are trying to do is not going to work."

"Oh, I wouldn't bet on that," Miss Charlene said, her face smug.

But then she changed her look. "Although you're probably right. Probably you'll just not take the quilt, and nothing will ever come of it. And you'll die a lonely old man, never knowing what you missed because you wouldn't take the quilt today."

Nolt shook his head, and he didn't mean to laugh, but he couldn't keep from smiling, although he didn't roll his eyes. "I'll take the quilt. I'll give it to my sister's friend, and I'll come out, unchanged." He shook his head. "Anything to make you ladies happy. After all, you guys do an awful lot for this town. Far be it for me to try to put a roadblock in your plans."

"Well, if you're not really blocking our plans, ask her out while you're there."

Nolt laughed outright at that. "That would be like dating my sister. Don't make me go there."

He shifted the box, grabbing the doorknob as Miss Charlene said, "Your sister is an adult woman, in case you haven't noticed."

"She's a kid. Wet behind the ears." He didn't really mean it. He knew his sister was an adult, and she definitely was more mature than what he gave her credit for sometimes, but there was a big difference between a twenty-two-year-old and a thirty-four-year-old. A lot of differences in life experiences, a lot of differences in maturity and wisdom.

He wanted a woman who matched his life level, not one who was just starting out, stars in her eyes and all of her interest devoted to having a good time.

He'd been in his twenties once, and he knew how it was.

The apartment Shasta rented was over the new bookstore, and although he'd never been up in it, he knew where it was and the door to get to it. Which was not locked.

Walking up the stairs, he wondered if he shouldn't have gotten her phone number and called first. It was Monday morning, just before noon on the Fourth of July. Would she be out celebrating?

He doubted it. She was more likely working.

Although, if she were painting something for someone, like the mailbox she did for Sadie, she probably did that at home. Wouldn't she? He had no idea, and he really didn't need to know.

Although her painting had been gorgeous, and there had been something about the girl herself that had been interesting to him.

Probably because he'd seen her once before, and she'd matured some since then. Nothing more than that. Although the cough that she had had concerned him. Which is why he wanted to make sure she had money over the weekend.

He didn't know what her circumstances were, but moving was expensive, and if she needed to go to the doctor, he wanted her to be able to afford to.

That was just him watching out for anyone, not because Shasta was special.

Because she wasn't.

Although he definitely could see a resemblance between her and Alana, the girl who'd chosen someone else.

That was not a point in her favor, though.

He turned at the top of the stairs and rapped on the door to Shasta's apartment.

As the echo in the hall quieted, he could hear what sounded like weak coughing from inside.

If she hadn't gone to the doctor, he was going to give her a hard time about it. There was something odd about that cough; it was more than just a regular run-of-the-mill cough a person got when they had a cold.

It could be bronchitis.

He stood waiting, but the door didn't open. Although the coughing stopped. Maybe she hadn't heard him.

He rapped again.

That time, he heard a faint, "It's open," before the coughing started again.

She didn't lock her door?

The thought irritated him, though he wasn't sure he could explain exactly why. It wasn't like Sweet Water was a hotbed of crime. It just seemed like a single woman living alone would be smarter than that.

Maybe he opened the door a little faster than he needed to, but he didn't slam it shut. Because his eyes had already scanned the room, over the box he was carrying, and saw what he assumed was Shasta, lying on the floor.

He would have set the box on the kitchen table, except there wasn't one.

So he just let it drop to the floor and walked straight through to the second room of the apartment. There were only two.

This was supposed to be the bedroom, he supposed, but there was no bed. Just the slender body of a young girl stretched out on the floor, with a towel under her head.

"Shasta?" he asked, concerned. Something that felt strangely like guilt tightened in his stomach.

He should have made Sadie check on her.

But Sadie had spent the weekend at Lark's, helping with her girls that she unofficially fostered and with her animals, and she probably hadn't thought of Shasta.

Nor had time to check on her.

But Nolt had. He just hadn't done it.

He'd known about the cough, known she was new in town, and known he should have followed up.

He knelt beside her, brushing her hair back away from her face so he could see the flushed cheeks and the red eyes that cracked as she felt his fingers.

"You're burning up."

"It's just warm in here. I haven't gotten the window open." Her voice was raspy, like she hadn't had a drink and had been on the floor for who knew how long.

"You never went to the doctor."

Before she could answer, her eyes rolled back in her head, and her lids closed.

"Shasta?" he said, touching her hair behind her ear and putting a hand on her shoulder, shaking gently.

He didn't have any medical training, but he was pretty sure she just passed out.

Or maybe she died.

The thought sent panic surging through him, and he grabbed her wrist, trying to remember where the pulse was.

Maybe it would be easier to feel it in her neck. He pressed his fingers there, and to his relief, he immediately felt her heartbeat. Weak, but it was there.

Sometimes it was faster to drive oneself to the ER, since it took a long time for an ambulance to come since it was all volunteer, but considering his pickup was at the garage, and he didn't want to leave Shasta here on the floor, he pulled his phone out of his pocket and dialed 911.

The operator, Agnes, was a friend of his from high school and assured him that an ambulance was on the way. It would be at least twenty minutes, though.

"I'll meet them down in front of her apartment door, right beside the new bookstore."

"Got it. I'll make sure they know."

He was almost positive she wasn't injured, although he looked for blood and gave a cursory examination of her body. No limbs twisted an odd way, just burning up with fever, and that cough that seemed to plague her even though she was unconscious, with weak spasms of her lungs.

He didn't think this was what bronchitis looked like. This looked more like something serious. Maybe pneumonia.

But it was July. People didn't get pneumonia in July.

Shifting, he put his arms under her body, lifting her and thinking she didn't weigh much.

It'd been a while since he lifted his sister for anything, but in his mind at least, she was a lot heavier than Shasta.

Which made him wonder exactly what was going on.

Maybe she was just naturally slender, but as he walked back through the apartment, with no furniture, save a chair, and no personal items, save the towel that had been under her head and a box of clothes that had been in the corner of the room, he wondered if there wasn't more to the story.

Maybe she wasn't eating because she couldn't afford to buy food.

He heard her say she hadn't been paid for a job that had taken her a month. And she hadn't turned down the cash.

The term *starving artist* came into his head, and it made him want to shake her, ask how bad things were.

It was just because his heart always went out for suffering. Not because there was anything special about Shasta.

He made it out of her apartment door okay, but carrying her down the narrow stairs without bumping her head on anything was difficult, especially since she was completely out and flopped against him like a rag doll.

Finally, he cradled her as closely as he could to his chest, using his elbow to support her head and actually dropping to one knee to support her body while he opened the door.

By the time he got her out, he was truly concerned. She hadn't woken up, hadn't moved at all other than to cough weakly.

If she'd been lying in her apartment like that all weekend, she was most definitely dehydrated, on top of being wracked with some kind of serious lung infection.

Pulling his phone out of his pocket, he called Sadie.

"Hello?" Sadie asked cheerfully. Her happiness was jarring after the seriousness of his thoughts.

"Hey. I have Shasta here, and she's not doing well at all. I was wondering if you could come and ride to the hospital with her."

"I can turn around. I'm on my way to Rockerton with Miss Teresa," Sadie said uncertainly. "Is she that bad?"

"I don't know." He didn't want to upset Sadie needlessly when he was no expert and really had no clue. Maybe she was just dehydrated, and a bag of liquids in an IV would bring her around.

He'd forgotten that Miss Teresa had called Sadie to take her to town.

He considered asking Sadie to turn around or at least meet them at Rockerton, but Miss Teresa truly didn't get out much, and maybe she really had been planning on getting Sadie to take her to town.

He hated to pull Sadie from that when he could go with Shasta himself.

Before he spoke, he heard Sadie say, as an aside, like she was talking to Miss Teresa, "He said that my friend Shasta is sick. Do you mind if we turn around?"

"I'll need to call my sister and tell her that we're not meeting her anymore."

Yeah. Nolt didn't want Miss Teresa to cancel her trip. They really did have something planned. "Never mind, Sadie. You go on. I'll stay with her. She'll just need you when you get back." And maybe her parents, too. He didn't want to alarm anyone needlessly...

"But I wasn't going to come back. Don't you remember? I took the week off, and I'm going on a ski trip with my friends in Colorado. I can cancel, but we've already paid for the house that we're renting. Although, if you can't stay with Shasta, I will."

"No. You go on." It was the first vacation that Sadie had taken since she'd gone to college. She was meeting her high school friends for a week of relaxing. She certainly deserved it, and he didn't want to take that from her.

"I can cancel my flight, but I know I won't get a refund. Maybe credit." Sadie obviously felt guilty.

"Sadie. Don't worry about it. I'll take care of her myself. You can take over when you get back. If she still needs it. I'm not sure what's wrong."

"I can't imagine. I roomed with her for four years in school, and I don't remember her ever being sick."

"Maybe she's just dehydrated. We'll see."

"Keep me posted," Sadie said.

"I will." Nolt swiped on his phone, looked up and down the street, and prayed that the ambulance would get there quickly.

Shifting Shasta, who hadn't moved, other than to cough weakly, he dialed his brother Calhoun's number.

Calhoun answered immediately. "Hello?"

"You mind bringing my pickup to the used bookstore in town?"

"I'm on it. What's up?" Sounds from the other end indicated Calhoun had moved and started walking.

"I delivered a quilt for the Piece Makers, and the girl who was supposed to get it was unconscious in her apartment. I'm going to make sure she gets to the hospital okay, since she's a friend of Sadie's and I promised her."

"Why isn't Sadie going?" Calhoun asked as a truck rumbled to life in the background.

"She has a ski trip."

"That's tomorrow."

"She's taking someone shopping today."

"I'll be right there," Calhoun said.

Nolt was relieved he didn't ask any more questions.

Like what was wrong with her and why Nolt hadn't called some other woman to go with her.

Valid questions.

But he'd promised Sadie he'd do it himself, and he hadn't even considered getting someone other than her.

Maybe there was a part of him that wanted to take care of this on his own.

He told himself it was because he had promised his sister, but he had a feeling that if he looked a little deeper, he'd find that he cared more than he wanted to admit. Which was weird, because he barely knew her.

Chapter 3

A lasting marriage must be a marriage of three - the bride,
the groom, and Christ in the center.
- Jill Tatum

"Are you sure she's safe to go home?" Nolt asked one more time.

Shasta didn't roll her eyes. She wasn't even tempted to. She appreciated him looking after her, but the anxiety in her chest threatened to push out.

Until the doctor nodded his head.

She breathed a sigh of relief but didn't allow it to be audible, because she didn't want Nolt to know how badly she absolutely could not stay in the hospital another second.

"As long as there's someone there to take care of her. And we'll have home nursing come in to check on her. She's insisting she needs to go, and I'm reluctant to let her." He looked over at her once more, his kindly old eyes crinkled below his bushy white brows and the sparse amount of white hair on his head.

He was a North Dakota man, and while he probably realized from her Midwestern accent that she wasn't native to North Dakota, he was obviously used to working with people who didn't want to stay in the hospital.

The doctor's eyes rested on Nolt. "And you said you were going to stay with her."

Nolt nodded, and Shasta tried not to squirm. She had no idea why he'd insisted on not leaving her the entire time she'd been in the hospital.

Several days' worth of beard growth attested to the fact that he'd kept his word.

Although he had gone to the truck stop down the road to shower, but only when the nurses had needed privacy with her.

She wasn't even sure he left to eat. She hadn't seen him anyway. If he had, he waited until she'd been sleeping, which she'd been doing a lot of.

"All right. She's probably not going to have much of an appetite for a week or two, but try to get her to drink as much broth and liquids as possible, even something like a powdered protein drink, just to get some nutrients in her. But don't force the food. Her appetite will come back." The doctor looked back down at his paper. "Make sure you take your medicine, every bit of it, even if you're feeling better before it runs out."

She nodded. She'd already heard all of this. And she figured the nurses would probably want to go over it again before she left. Not that she'd been in the hospital that much, but in one of the foster families she'd grown up in, she had a foster sibling who had been in and out of hospitals. Neither of them had stayed in that foster home long.

It was exceptionally hard to find someone who wanted to foster a teenager, let alone a teenager with medical issues.

The doctor went over a few more things, then told her he'd have her discharge papers ready and the nurses would be in for her signature and to go over them.

Again.

She felt weak, exhausted really, and the doctor had been right, she had no appetite.

But at least her cough was mostly gone.

Nolt moved to the side of the bed and reached down. "I have some clean clothes. If you want to try sitting up, I can help you to the restroom if that's where you want to change." He paused. "If you can change by yourself?"

It was pretty obvious he didn't want to help her, and maybe it wasn't quite as obvious, but she definitely did not want his help. The nurses had been so busy today. She hated to bother them again.

It had been awkward enough having him there. Brooding. Almost angry looking.

That wasn't true. He never looked angry. But he wasn't one of those people who went around cheering everyone up wherever he went.

Definitely his bedside manner could use some improvement.

But she wasn't going to be the one to tell him that.

She reached her hand out after she sat up, trying not to look like she was waiting for the world to quit whirling around her before she stood.

"I'll carry them. I'll give them to you once you're there." It was like he knew she was fighting just to stay conscious. She had no idea how she was going to change clothes. "Are you sure you want to leave? You look like you can barely stand up, and... I don't want to see anything happen to you."

"Because I'm Sadie's friend?" she couldn't help but ask. Because his words made her stomach turn. She'd always had a crush on him, and it hadn't gotten any better knowing that he was here taking care of her. But he'd mentioned Sadie once or twice, although this was the first time she flat-out asked about her.

There just hadn't been a whole lot of time to talk, since she'd been sleeping so much.

"Yeah," he said, his face serious, concern in his eyes as he watched her movements.

Yeah. That's what she thought. She didn't want his attention because he felt obligated to give it.

She wanted to shove it back, but she couldn't do this on her own, and she had no one else to help her.

She had a few friends in Nebraska where she'd grown up with her different foster parents, but once she turned eighteen, she aged out, and the last ones she had weren't the lovey-dovey kind of parents who would tell her she could stay as long as she wanted to, like some of her foster friends had. Those kinds of parents were few and far between, and she had the normal kind. The ones that kicked her out as soon as their checks from the state stopped coming.

At least she had gone to college for free.

She really shouldn't complain, because she knew Sadie had a mountain of debt she was paying because of her college education.

She supposed that could have been her. But it might have been a fair trade-off if she would have had parents to fall back on.

Or a dad at least, like Sadie had. And a bunch of big brothers.

She slid a glance at Nolt, who stood beside her bed, waiting for her to stand, like he was getting ready to catch her but wouldn't touch her until it was absolutely necessary.

Yeah. She had to get better, so she wouldn't be beholden to him anymore.

No matter how hard she might be crushing on him, she didn't want to owe him so much.

Plus, a crush was different than actually liking someone because they were kind and funny and considerate and sweet.

Taking a breath, pulling up all the inner reserves she had, she pushed off the bed and stood. One hand behind her, clutching the back of her hospital gown.

They hadn't gotten any more modest since her foster sister had been in the hospital.

She wasn't sure whether she was clutching it in a way that it was actually covering anything, or whether it just looked like she was eighty years old and had a bad back.

Still, at least she was making the effort.

"Stubborn." Nolt's words came out beside her ear, just a split second before his arms went behind her back and knees and swooped her off the floor.

"Determined. It's much nicer," she said, panting. She hadn't realized how weak she was.

The doctor had said he wouldn't let her go home if he didn't think she could handle it, but he had also said that she would have to be very careful and not do anything for herself.

She supposed that included getting dressed.

"I don't think you should be leaving here." His words were not tender and sweet but a low growl in her ear.

"I need to." That's all she could say.

He grunted but thankfully didn't argue. "I know you're not going to like this, but there's no way you're putting these clothes on by yourself. So don't fight me, because I'm helping you."

Like she could fight him. She felt like she was going to throw up and pass out at the same time.

But she couldn't just give in. She heaved a sigh, like she was really put out, and said, "Fine. Help. Just close your eyes."

He set her gently on the floor. "They're closed."

She wasn't so weak that she couldn't spot a lie when she heard one, and she looked slowly over her shoulder, careful so she didn't make her head spin. "They're not."

"They were when I said it. I just opened them right away. Now, put your leg in these, and we'll wait to take the gown off until we've got them on and buttoned. That's the best I can do."

She appreciated that small concession for modesty. He could have insisted on sweeping the gown off right away, because it did get in the way as she held onto him tightly and barely lifted her foot off the floor while he pulled one of her pant legs over her foot.

He kept a close eye on her as he pulled it up and then said, "Lift."

With both hands on his shoulders and teeth gritted, she held her other foot up while he put her pant leg over her foot.

"You forgot my underwear," she ground out.

"It was a deliberate elimination on my part. If we can get a shirt and pants on you, we'll be doing well."

She supposed that meant no bra. That probably shouldn't upset her as much as it did.

But she didn't argue, although she did turn her back to him as the gown came off, and a shirt went over her head.

"I think you'll be sweltering in this, but I couldn't find any shorts in your apartment."

"Is there a sweatshirt?"

"It's July. I don't think you need a sweatshirt."

"I'm cold."

"I'll get you one as soon as I can. I didn't bring one, and in hindsight, I guess it makes sense that you'd be cold. You've been sick." He put his arms around her back and her legs and swept her off the floor again. "Snuggle with me. I'll keep you as warm as I can."

She was too tired to argue, too tired to hold on to him even, so she just allowed him to cradle her against him and pressed her head against his hard chest.

He smelled good, like strength and responsibility and the wild North Dakota wind.

Like nighttime in Nebraska, in the spring when the corn shot out of the ground, and everything was damp and new and the stars lit the sky in brilliant sparkles, and the world seemed alive with promise and new birth and opportunities, and she had the nerve to reach out and go for what she wanted.

She almost snorted. That wasn't a good scent. Because look where it had gotten her. Hospitalized, with a bill she definitely could not pay, since she couldn't even afford to feed herself.

She kept her head on Nolt's chest as a nurse came in with her paperwork, listening with half an ear to the instructions.

At some point, she had stopped caring whether she lived or died. Probably shortly after she collapsed in her apartment. She just wanted the terrible coughing to stop.

And for the most part, it had. Some of her medication helped with that. She wasn't sure which one, but that was the only one she cared that she took.

Her stomach still hurt, and her ribs were sore from all the coughing.

After the nurse left, assuring her that there would be someone with a wheelchair to come take her down to the front door, Nolt looked at her and said, "I'm gonna go get my pickup and bring it around to the front. If they come to get you, don't let them take you until I'm back. Okay?"

"Can we meet you down at the front?" she asked, the words coming hard.

"I'd rather do it myself. And I think you'll thank me, if you've seen what I've seen."

Despite herself, she smiled a little, unsure whether he actually meant to make that a joke, or whether it had come out accidentally.

She didn't even look to see if he was smiling. Probably not. He seemed taciturn and serious.

But he'd been gentle every time he touched her.

Almost too gentle. She wanted him to be impersonal, just get it done, but instead he made sure he was considerate of her and careful.

No one had come for her by the time he came back, slightly breathless, and she wondered if he'd run.

The thought made her smile. Not because it was sweet, but because it was so ludicrous. He had run.

She wasn't sure why he was here, other than feeling like Sadie couldn't, so he needed to be. But he didn't care so much that he would make sure that he didn't miss a second with her. Although, in her fanciful brain, she wouldn't have minded believing that.

They didn't have to wait long after that for the wheelchair to arrive, and Nolt didn't even ask, just picked her up and set her in it.

She didn't have the strength to argue, although she didn't have the sense to not. So it was probably a good thing she was too tired. She could see he was right; she needed him.

Rather than resenting everything he did, she tried to set her brain on appreciation. Even if he was just doing it for his sister, she could appreciate it.

"Thank you," she murmured.

"What?" he said as he was straightening, stooping back down and looking into her eyes.

"Thank you," she said, trying to make it come out stronger, but it was just louder.

He didn't move for just a moment, and she realized, in the two days she'd been in the hospital, that was the first time she'd thanked him.

"My pleasure," he finally murmured, and she wasn't sure what to make of that. He hadn't said "you're welcome." It was "my pleasure."

Deciding she wasn't going to try to analyze it, she listened while Nolt told the sweet lady who'd arrived to roll her out of the hospital that he was going to be doing it.

The lady nodded, and before she left, she patted Shasta's hand. "You have yourself a nice man there, honey." She squeezed slightly before letting go. "I was married for over fifty years to a nasty fellow who wouldn't even have been here, and I would have had to beg him to pick me up. You ought to treat that one right."

It was odd to hear anything negative come out of such a sweet old lady's mouth, but she supposed if she were married to someone who wouldn't even come to the hospital to pick her up or wouldn't stay in the hospital when she needed him, she'd not have anything nice to say about him, either.

She squeezed the lady's hand back and nodded. She was too tired to argue. So she didn't tell her that he wasn't her husband, not even close, barely an acquaintance, and he was only doing it because he told his sister he would.

There was no need to get into all of that. The fact of the matter was, Nolt was a good man. And she should appreciate him.

Even if she wished things were different. She couldn't change it, so she had to let it go. That was life, just accepting what God gave you. Because there were things you couldn't change.

Like being a foster kid.

Like having pneumonia.

Like having the man you crushed on consider you an obligation he was taking care of for his sister.

She dozed off and on on the way home, and again he didn't ask when he pulled up to the sidewalk but came around, unbuckled her seatbelt, and carried her up to her apartment, using a key to unlock the door.

"Where?" she asked, her voice thready and her body feeling like it was made of lead. The ride home had taken her last ounce of energy.

"Out of your purse. I would have asked you if I could go through it, but you weren't exactly awake."

He was right, and she wasn't upset. Not until he opened the door and walked through.

Her bare apartment had been transformed.

There was a kitchen table with four chairs. A refrigerator. There had already been a stove, but now there was a microwave above it, and it looked like it had been cleaned.

Nolt did not stop in the kitchen but walked through to the second room.

She gave a weak gasp as she saw the bed and a dresser. A beautiful quilt lay over the bed, and she assumed that was the quilt he'd brought when he found her on the floor. She thought she remembered him mentioning it in the hospital at some point.

He set her down on her feet, standing, but keeping one, then two, hands on her shoulders as he straightened.

She wanted him to go, needed him to leave. Because...

"Why are you crying?" he asked, and it sounded a little rough, like he was annoyed.

She hadn't made a sound, hadn't wanted him to know, because then she would have to explain.

But the sick feeling in her stomach twisted, and the silent tears that flowed down her face didn't stop but multiplied. She pulled both lips in and crossed her arms over her chest, hugging herself and trying not to give in to the despair that threatened to overwhelm her.

Chapter 4

*Besides love I tell my daughter 2 things--pick your battles
and don't sweat the small stuff. I have been married 54 years
so I know it works.*
- Diane F. Bookwalter from PA

"Are you hurt?" Nolt asked, his voice not as dispassionate as before. In fact, he sounded a little panicked.

Shasta shook her head.

"Then what's wrong?" he asked, more forcefully this time, like he expected an answer, and now.

Her voice was going to come out all squeaky, but she couldn't help it. He didn't understand.

"I can't afford this. I'm never going to be able to pay for all this. I can't afford the hospital, I can't afford...this!"

If she had enough energy, she would throw herself across the bed, but as it was, she just slowly crumpled and would have ended up in a pile on the floor if Nolt hadn't reached out and grabbed her, doing what now must be familiar as he put an arm behind her knees and one behind her back.

He held her there, taking a step toward the bed. But he stopped and held her suspended over it for a moment, like he was going to set her down, before he seemed to change his mind and cradled her closer, turning while he sat on the bed. And held her close.

"Stop. Don't cry. You don't want to get all stuffed up again. Then you'll start to cough, and then I'll have to take you back to the hospital."

"I'll cry if I want to," she mumbled.

Not sounding forceful, but she meant it. He wasn't going to tell her not to cry. It was her prerogative, and she needed to. She couldn't do anything else; she was too weak. Crying was the only outlet.

"You don't have to pay for any of this. It's been donated. It's not new." His voice was calm, quiet, caring. She didn't want any of that right now. She just wanted military precision, someone to do what needed to be done and leave so she could curl up into a big ball of self-pity and cry as long as she needed to.

"I can't accept any of this. It's too much."

"People wanted to give it. I wouldn't look the gift horse in the mouth too much, anyway, because I'm pretty sure this bed came from Mrs. Palmer's attic, and it's probably been there since before the first world war."

"Then it's good quality," she said, not sobbing but the tears still flowing.

He grunted. "That's probably true, but it's as old as the hills, older. In fact, she probably had it packed right beside the Conestoga wagon that her ancestors came out west on."

"I could paint that," she said, her eyes closed, a little smile on her face along with the tears.

"You sure could. You'd make it look beautiful." His voice was soft, and his hand came up and stroked her hair back away from her face.

It felt so gentle, and she wanted to lean into it. There hadn't been too many times in her life where she'd felt the gentle stroke of someone's hand, and far from making her feel better, it made her tears start flowing harder.

"Hey. Quit that," Nolt said, making her smile again. Obviously, he didn't have much experience in comforting anyone. Her tears made him nervous.

She couldn't help it. She already owed for the hospital stay, and now for furniture, and all the money she had in the world was the money that Nolt had given her Friday evening and twenty dollars in a bank account.

"It doesn't matter how old it is, I can't take it."

"You can. I'm telling you, people donated because they wanted to, not because anyone was holding a gun to their head, or because they wanted you to owe them. They gave it freely. And, someday, when you're back on your feet, you can return the gesture. Either to them or someone else."

"I owe you." She didn't want to look him in the eye, and she hadn't the strength to wipe her tears away, and she didn't have a tissue to blow her nose. All negative. She tried to stop the negative thoughts and think about something happy.

"You don't. I promise you. You don't owe me anything."

"You've been off work for the last two days. I owe you that. Plus, there hasn't been a thing that I've needed that you haven't made sure I've gotten. Including a ride home and being carried up the stairs just now."

She would have said more, but she was already out of breath.

"Don't get yourself worked up."

"Don't tell me what to do!" she snapped. Then regretted it immediately.

Here she was, telling him how much she owed him, and how did she pay him back? By being mean. And snapping at him.

"Sorry." She took a breath and sniffed. "Thank you. Thank you for all you've done. I will repay you."

"Just do something nice to somebody else. Or maybe someday down the road, I'll need something. Remember me."

It couldn't be that easy. Even foster parents got money. As nice as some of them were, they still got paid. She couldn't expect him to do all the things that he'd done without her paying him back.

"Now, I'm going to pull the covers down on your bed, and I'm gonna set you in it. Unless you have to use the restroom first?"

She almost shook her head no, but she did have to go, and...as much as she hated to admit it, she probably couldn't do it by herself. She wasn't sure she could even walk to the restroom without help. For the first time, she wondered if maybe she should have stayed in the hospital.

Nevertheless, she said, "I need to go."

In the hospital, there had always been a nurse to help her, but now he carried her to the restroom, and she tried not to die of humiliation as he helped her and held her steady with one hand as he pulled her pants down with the other.

"I'm glad Orchid picked out stretchy pants. It would take twice as long if I had to unbutton them."

She couldn't talk. Maybe getting naked in front of people was something that didn't bother the rest of the world, but it wasn't something she normally did, and it was made even worse by the fact that it was Nolt who was helping her. She didn't want to look sick and weak in front of him.

She did what needed to be done quickly and was slightly surprised by the time they were pulling her pants back up that she hadn't died of embarrassment.

He didn't seem bothered at all. Of course. It wasn't him that was too weak to use the restroom by himself.

She imagined things would be a little different if the tables were turned, but if they were, she would appreciate his good attitude, so she did her best.

"Thank you," she said, her eyes closed as he swooped her back up and carried her to the bed.

"My pleasure," he said, and she cracked her eyes, because she was pretty sure there was a hint of humor in his voice.

"Really?" she murmured.

"I was the oldest of six brothers. Granted, I never had to help them go to the bathroom, but I cleaned up my share of messes involving liquids leaked from the body as each new baby came along and became a toddler. I promise you, I would much rather do it with a beautiful young woman, who at least gets the liquid in the right spot, than chase after a muddy, dirty toddler who's already smeared the stuff that has come out of his rear end all over the side of his bedroom wall."

Her lips had turned up into a grin, and she didn't even bother to try to stop them, although she didn't open her eyes. "You make what we just did sound almost fun."

He'd called her beautiful. Maybe he didn't mean it, and she knew she wasn't supposed to take it to heart.

Instead, she tried to focus on what he said: things could have been a lot worse.

"You keep giving me compliments like that, and you're gonna turn my head." She wasn't even sure what she meant by that, but in her weakened state, it almost felt like flirting.

It seemed like that was what he was doing.

"Telling you you're a good girl for putting all your pee in the potty?" he asked, like he didn't know what she was talking about.

"No, no, no, no." She had trouble keeping her eyes open and her mind focused. But she knew what he said. "You called me beautiful." She said it like she caught him red-handed stealing money out of her purse.

"Surely not."

"You did. You can't take it back."

"I don't recall saying that. I'm afraid you're going to have to prove it."

"I don't have to prove it. I said it happened, so it did."

"Just because you're beautiful doesn't mean I'm going to tell you that. And you can't make me."

That time, she opened her eyes, and they grinned together.

"It's good to be home. Thanks." Even if her apartment didn't feel like home, and even if she had no idea how she was going to pay for everything, it was nice not to be in the hospital anymore. To be in her own space.

"It's great that you stopped leaking. Out of both ends," he added. But his words were belied by the gentle brush of his thumb on her skin as he swiped the tears off her cheeks.

Tucking the quilt around her, he said, "Are you hungry?"

She shook her head. Not opening her eyes, because she didn't want him to see what his touch had done to her. Caring, consideration, and the touch of another human. They weren't things she was used to. Then, to have him telling her she was beautiful on top of it.

If she wasn't already crushing on him, she would have started.

"Do you want me to get you a drink?" he asked.

"That would be great, but you don't have to do it this second."

Just the little bit that they'd just done had completely exhausted her, and while she was thirsty, she was more tired than anything.

"Hang on. Let me get you a little something, then you can take a rest. Okay?"

"Yeah."

Nolt left for a bit and came back, slipping his hand around the back of her head. "I'm going to lift you up a little bit, just so we don't spill it everywhere. I have a cup. Can you see it?"

"Yeah."

He guided it to her mouth, and she drank, more than she thought she would. She hadn't realized how thirsty she was. Maybe, when she woke up, she'd be hungry, but it just felt good to feel the cool liquid sliding down her throat.

Except, she was back to being cold.

He laid her head back down on the pillow and slipped his hand out.

"Are you shivering?"

"Sorry. The water was cold."

He disappeared from beside her, and she just lay there, thinking in a minute or two when she got rested, she'd roll over on her side and curl up. But for the time being, she just shivered and tried to not think about how cold she was.

Just a few seconds later, the side of the bed shifted beside her, and his body, warm and hard, slid in next to her.

"Turn on your side, and I'll warm you from the back."

She took a breath and then obeyed, summoning up the last of her energy.

It had been exhausting coming home from the hospital. Her limbs felt like dead weights, and it took all of her energy just to breathe.

Still, she wasn't dead, and the warmth behind her felt good. The hardness and strength, the hand that wrapped around her stomach, and the arm that went under her head. She felt sheltered and secure. Cared for, and like someone cared.

Which were two different things in her book.

Her foster parents could care for her and not really care about her. It felt like Nolt was not just caring for her but cared about her.

In the back of her head, she reminded herself that he was only doing this for his sister, but maybe there was a little part of him that was doing it because he wanted to.

She held onto that thought. Somehow, it made everything okay to think that while maybe he didn't love her exactly, he at least liked her, and that's why he was here. Not out of a sense of charity or a sense of obligation.

With those thoughts, she fell asleep with a smile on her face.

Chapter 5

Communication is Key.
- Jodi Wresh from Minnesota

"I win!" Shasta called out, slapping down the last card and giving Nolt a triumphant grin.

Nolt returned it. "That's the first game you won today. So go ahead and enjoy it."

"Wow. Rub it in when someone's down." She grabbed the cards and started shuffling.

He handed her the box and moved the tray that Silas had made in his shop for Shasta off the bed, leaning it against the nightstand.

"It's not my fault you had a losing streak three hours long." He stood, stretching.

"I still think you were cheating. I just can't prove it. Nobody wins that much."

"When you use your brain, crazy things happen."

She didn't have a comeback for that one, so she stuck her tongue out at him.

He was a little tempted to stick his tongue back out at her too, but instead of doing that, he grabbed her tongue between his thumb and finger.

"Hey, give that back!"

At least that's what he thought she said. It was a little hard for her to form words when he was holding her tongue.

"Keep that thing in your mouth where it belongs. Didn't your mom ever teach you any better?"

Like she always did when he brought up anything about her childhood, she turned her eyes away.

Although, when he let go of her tongue, she wiped it off with her hand like her hand was somehow cleaner than his fingers.

In the past week, she'd gotten better, sleeping less and being awake more. They started playing games and found themselves pretty evenly matched. Although today he had had a rather large winning streak, and he hadn't been cheating. Which Shasta knew. He'd found out that she was an honest player as well, which he liked.

Actually, he found that he really enjoyed spending time with her.

"Thanks for coming today," she said, in a totally different tone than the happy one she'd been using. More subdued.

"Of course. You're kind of in my schedule now."

"Not anymore. The home nurse said I was good to go."

She'd finished up all her medicine, and while she hadn't gotten out of bed and done any cooking, she'd been able to get up and do everything that needed to be done in the bathroom by herself. Which was a relief to her, he was sure.

He had taken a few days off work, but even the last two since he'd gone back, he'd come and spent the evenings and nights with her.

She'd done a lot of sleeping though, and he hadn't gotten to talk to her much.

A good thing, since every second he'd spent with her had seemed to make him want to spend more time with her. Be more interested in what she was interested in and make plans to do things with her after she got up.

Which was weird.

He thought he was doing this for his sister Sadie, since Shasta was her friend, and he said he would, but he found he was doing it because he wanted to.

"You ready to see what Louise brought for supper?" he asked as she carefully put the cards back in the box.

"Not only am I ready to see, I'm going to eat at the table tonight."

"Don't overdo," he said. She was sitting up in bed just fine, but she had been taking her meals on her tray.

"I want to. The auction is the night after tomorrow, and I want to go."

"And everyone wants you there, so maybe you should conserve your energy." He watched with concern as she stood up. Although he didn't know why. She'd been getting up by herself for several days now, just fine.

Maybe it was having seen her crumple to the ground when he'd first brought her home. Or seeing her passed out on the floor. He just...knew how sick she had been.

"I'm building my strength. It's not until the day after tomorrow. I want to move around. I'm tired of being stuck here. Although..." Her grateful eyes landed on him. "I really do appreciate your company. Even if you do cheat at cards."

He laughed, shaking his head. He wasn't going to allow her to annoy him by telling him he was cheating when they both knew he wasn't.

She moved through the bedroom to the kitchen, and he followed, not putting his hands out behind her but wanting to.

She was right. The auction was in her name, hastily put together by the citizens of Sweet Water to help pay her hospital bills.

There would be music and dancing, and people were donating items to be auctioned off. Word of the auction had gone around all the small communities surrounding Sweet Water, and people were coming for miles.

They even had someone who had donated an antique, fully restored Mustang to be sold. It was garnering a lot of interest. He and his brothers were donating several items through their trucking company, and there were tons of crafts and baked goods.

The auction started at three in the afternoon, and from the looks of the things that were being gathered, since they were all being collected at his family's garage, it was going to take hours to get through it all.

There was even talk of having two separate auctions. Household and baked goods and farm and auto.

"I was actually hoping I would feel well enough tomorrow to make something for the auction."

Ladies were bringing covered dishes to feed everyone, and he and his brothers were donating soft drinks and water.

"It's for you. You don't have to do anything for it."

She turned around with her mouth open. They'd had that discussion before. How she had such a hard time accepting everything that everyone was doing.

He thought it had to do with her upbringing, but she clammed up both times he asked.

He could take a hint. She didn't want to talk about it.

"Looks like some kind of pasta casserole. It smells delicious," Shasta said as she pulled the cover off.

Nolt grabbed plates and set them on the table. But he hesitated with his hand on the silverware drawer when Shasta's phone buzzed.

He knew Sadie was on her way home, and surprisingly, he had been hoping that she wouldn't make it before supper.

He wasn't sure why, but he'd been looking forward to eating with Shasta one last time. And when she got up and went to the table, he'd been even more excited about it.

Probably because today was the last day he'd be spending with Shasta, since Sadie would be home.

He could admit to himself that he was going to miss her. She'd been fun and happy and funny too.

"If we wait a few minutes, Sadie will be here. She said she's just pulling into town." Shasta spoke while still facing the counter, so he couldn't see her face, but maybe it was just his imagination that she sounded almost as disappointed as he felt.

Maybe she was unhappy for their time together to be over. It was just as well.

"I wanted to thank you," he started. Not having planned to really say anything, but feeling like maybe he wouldn't get another opportunity.

"Thank me?" she said, turning around with the casserole in her hands.

She walked to the table, setting it down, then waited for him to answer.

He tried to gather his thoughts. He wasn't always the best at voicing things, and he didn't want to give her the wrong idea, although he honestly wasn't sure what that was, but he wanted her to know...

"You could have had a really bad attitude. You could have made things miserable for everyone. You had a pretty hard time, and I know some of the things that happened were tough for you."

He fingered the fork in his hand before setting it carefully down on the table.

"Instead, for the time you were awake anyway," he said, just to get her to smile and to kind of lighten the air, because it was feeling too heavy and oppressive. He was getting too serious, and he didn't want that. "I had a good time. You're fun. You weren't always comfortable, but you were always considerate and not demanding. I'm actually going to miss you, kid." He lightened up on that last sentence and ruffled her hair, just like he would have ruffled his sister's hair.

He wasn't fooling himself. Because he didn't feel the same way about Shasta that he felt about his sister.

What he felt made him uncomfortable, not just because of the big age difference, but because when he fell in love with Alana, and she'd chosen someone else, he never thought he would think of anyone that way again. He had wanted to, but he wasn't really the kind of man who jumped from woman to woman.

He put down roots, and they grew deep.

But Shasta had shaken his root system, if that was the right analogy.

"You're trying to say you like me," she said, flashing him a grin.

After the first few days in the hospital, where maybe she'd been a little intimidated by him, he wasn't sure, or maybe she had just been so sick she didn't have enough energy to laugh and joke, she'd become more like herself and had fun teasing him.

It was a little bit weird, because while his brothers weren't afraid to make fun of him, it was not a light, happy thing.

And Sadie, whom he loved with all of his heart, had a deep respect for him and didn't joke with him much.

"Maybe. Maybe not. It depends on whether or not you're calling me a cheater right now or not," he shot back. That was another thing about Shasta, she helped him find his lighter side.

No one else got to see that side.

"If I call you a cheater, you like me."

"Whoa. You've got that backward."

"Okay. How about we argue about this after we eat, so we don't give Sadie a bad impression."

"You want me to fake-like you while Sadie's here?"

"Yeah. I don't want to ruin my good reputation with her. She thinks I'm amazing."

He almost said "that's because you are," but he didn't.

"She never did have very good sense when it came to judging people," he said instead.

Chapter 6

Love and trust.
- Kendra Muonio from Battle Ground, Washington

S hasta laughed as Nolt had known she would. They'd just developed a rapport where neither one of them took the other one seriously, and they didn't get offended. It wasn't a rapport that he had with any other person, and he kind of liked it. Where he didn't have to weigh his words all the time or worry that he was going to do something that was going to upset her.

Not that he went around concerned about that kind of thing all the time, it was just relaxing to be with someone who was not easily offended. In fact, he'd almost found it was impossible to offend her.

He hoped to have been the same way for her. He wanted to ask, because he'd had such a good time with her and hoped she had the same experience with him.

"You know, all joking aside, I'm going to miss you. You've been...amazing. And I know it was because you promised your sister you'd take care of me so that she could still go on her trip, and I admit I resented that a little bit at first, because I didn't want you doing what you are doing out of a sense of duty. Mostly because you were doing it so well, and I felt so cared for. And it felt wrong to feel so cared for when you didn't really care. If that makes sense."

"Um, you're talking like a girl," he said.

She laughed. "Never mind. I just appreciate what you've done. And I'm sorry if I had a bad attitude at the beginning."

"That's okay. You were pretty sick. I didn't mind. I mean, you yelled at me and everything, but I didn't mind. You can pay for that along with the rest."

"Wait. You said I didn't owe you. Now you're going to make me pay?"

"Sure. You're going to clean my house for free for the next five years. Right?"

"I don't think so. But..." Her eyes brightened. "I will paint your walls if you want me to."

"Flowers?" he asked, with his brows raised, saying the word "flowers" so she understood that he was a man, and he didn't have flowers on his wall.

Not unless he had a wife living in his house that was making him have flowers on his wall.

"I can paint other things."

"Okay. As long as it's not flowers."

"Hearts. I think you're a heart guy."

"Never mind."

"Ogres? Or little devils? Unicorns?"

"This is getting worse."

"The man doesn't appreciate anything," she said, sighing like she was really put out.

"The woman is being unreasonable."

"Painting your walls pink with purple unicorns and orange candy canes would be unreasonable."

"See? She's the expert on being unreasonable."

"I think the man complains too much."

"I think the woman is the one complaining."

He hadn't done it on purpose, but he'd taken a couple of steps toward her, and she'd done the same thing, so they weren't exactly nose to nose because he was a good bit taller than she was, but they were within arm's distance of each other, and he didn't mind the closeness at all. In fact, he wouldn't mind being even closer.

"The woman is not complaining. She's just pointing out the facts. Since the man seems to be unable to see them on his own."

"The man can see just fine. It was the woman that wasn't able to see. Which is why the man—"

"You guys are talking to each other in third person? Don't you think that's weird?"

Nolt jerked his head toward the door. He hadn't heard it open. But Sadie stood there, one hand on her hip, one hand still on the doorknob, and her face scrunched up like she wasn't quite sure what was going on in the kitchen, but she knew it was something very, very odd.

"Sadie!" Shasta said like they hadn't just been talking to each other in third person and she called them on it. She hurried over to the door, giving her friend a hug.

Sadie hugged her back, but over her shoulder, she met Nolt's eyes, her brows raised in a silent but very clear "What in the world is going on in here?" way.

Nolt looked away for a moment, then he lifted his arms, hands in an "I'm innocent" gesture.

Sadie flattened her mouth and pulled it back, clearly saying she didn't believe him.

He didn't have a chance to answer, because Shasta pulled back. "I hope you had a good trip."

"I did. We had a lot of fun. Although, I did feel guilty the whole time because I knew you didn't know anyone in town, and while Nolt had promised me that he would take care of you, sometimes the way men take care of things isn't the way it should be done."

"Hey. I resent that. Also, I'm standing right here," Nolt said, in a very big brotherly fashion.

"We can see you easily," Sadie said calmly, but her eyes were narrowed a little, as though she were thinking.

Nolt, having seen that look on her face when she was a toddler about to use the toilet as a swimming pool for her Barbie dolls, racked his brain for something to say that would take her mind off whatever it was that she was thinking.

"Shasta and I were just talking about the auction that we're having Saturday night. Did you see the garage?"

"No. I...drove right here. But I can see that you two have everything under control, so I think I'll go ahead and run back to the garage and see how Marigold's been doing with the paperwork. I'll check the auction stuff too. I'm guessing it needs to be organized."

"I thought you were staying for supper?"

Sadie took a breath and paused, almost as though she were thinking of an excuse. "I wish I could. But I just have a lot of stuff to do."

"You were taking over for me. I was going to do all that stuff."

"But it really needs a woman's hand, and you have everything under control here." Sadie grabbed Shasta and gave her one last quick hug. "I'm so glad to see you're up and around. The way Nolt talked, I thought I was going to be coming back to a half-decayed skeleton."

"That's gross," Nolt said automatically, but he felt like she could have come back to a funeral. The doctor actually said that she wouldn't have lasted another night on the floor of her apartment without medical intervention, and he couldn't believe she'd lasted as long as she had.

Maybe they said that to everyone so that patients appreciated the medical skills it took to bring her back from the brink of death, but Nolt had seen her that night and knew the doctor wasn't joking.

Shasta had been close to death.

"Okay. I'll see you around."

"Of course. We'll see each other at the auction if nowhere else. There's a lot of work to do to get ready for it, if I understand correctly." Sadie gave a little wave. "And with you doing so well here, I'm sure I'll have plenty of time to get everything straightened out."

Sadie slipped out the door, shutting it behind her.

"Right there's a good reason for you to lock your door," Nolt muttered.

Shasta burst out laughing.

But then she walked over to the table and sat down. "Whew! I'm tired. Maybe I should take supper in bed after all."

"Maybe that's for the best. You do look a little pale."

He tried not to worry, because she really was a lot better. And she was strong and young, like the doctor had said when he allowed her to go home. He wouldn't have allowed an elderly person who had had the same issues out of his sight, but since her age was in her favor, it hadn't been as much of a risk.

"I got the feeling she didn't want to stay," Shasta said, setting her elbow on the table and leaning her head on her hand.

"I don't think that had as much to do with you as it did with me." Nolt pulled a chair out and sat down in it, catty-corner from Shasta.

"Why would it have anything to do with you?" She didn't raise her head from her hand but still managed to tilt her head in inquiry.

How was he going to answer that without sounding very guilty?

He figured he'd just tell her the truth. "I think when she walked in, you and I were goofing off, and she got the wrong idea."

"The wrong idea?"

"Yeah. I think she thought there is more going on than what there was. It was just us goofing off, nothing else."

"Oh. Yeah. Right. Just goofing off. Nothing else."

Her voice sounded tired, and he looked again, wondering if maybe she'd really overdone it, with coming out to the kitchen and then the excitement of having Sadie back. Plus, he'd been goofing off with her and hadn't really been paying attention to her energy levels.

"I think I'm going to go lie down."

"What about eating?"

"That's okay. I'm not really hungry."

"Not this again," he said, just under his breath because he didn't want to make her feel guilty for not eating. But for the first few days she'd been home, it was all he could do to get her to drink some broth during the few hours she was awake during the day.

She didn't have any weight left to lose.

"No. I'm fine. Just..."

"Maybe you overdid it?" he suggested.

"Yeah. That's probably it. I think I overdid it."

He tried not to hover as she walked to her bed, pulling the covers back and lying down facing away from him.

She must have fallen asleep almost immediately, because he didn't see her move for a long time.

Chapter 7

First of all, you need to have God in your hearts. Learn to listen to each other no matter what.   Put God first and then each other. We will be married 49 years in Feb.
- Mary Lopp from Florida

"What was up yesterday between you and Nolt?" Sadie asked Shasta as they settled down at the table with a piece of egg custard in front of both of them.

People had been sending her food right and left. So much that she actually asked Nolt to help her get rid of it. There was no way she could eat everything people had been sending, and she hated for the food to go to waste.

She really was trying to eat as much as she could, because she knew she'd get her strength back faster, but she just didn't have much of an appetite.

"Nothing. He said he thought you suspected there was more going on than what there was."

"You were talking to each other in third person."

"Just goofing."

"He was smiling."

"He does that sometimes."

"Not often."

Shasta shrugged her shoulders.

"And he was...joking."

"He does that too. Surely you've heard him? He's your brother." Shasta didn't understand why Sadie was insisting on making a big deal about it, since Nolt obviously smiled and joked, and not just with her.

Surely.

"Nolt is serious all the time. He's the oldest. You know, the commander. Everybody looks to him and listens to him."

"Yeah, he does get a little bossy. But you just roll with it and move on."

She sliced her spoon down through the custard, loving how smooth and creamy it looked. And wishing she felt more like eating it.

Maybe her lack of appetite was more because Nolt and Sadie must have talked, because Sadie was here today and he wasn't.

She kept telling herself she wasn't disappointed, but it was an outright lie. She had been very disappointed this morning when she woke up and he was gone, and Sadie was sitting at the kitchen table, her laptop open in front of her, working on invoices from the company.

When Shasta had asked, carefully, if there had been a problem, Sadie had laughed and said her job was portable while Nolt's was not. Then she laughed again and said that Nolt was the oldest. He laid down the law.

Shasta wasn't sure what all of that meant, but one thing she did know, she missed Nolt.

Maybe that's what she'd been afraid of. Since she already had a huge crush on him, had for years, when he started to be nice to her, it wasn't that hard to fall a little deeper and then get hurt when he disappeared. After all, everyone knew there was a girl he was still stuck on from his high school days.

Which seemed a little unbelievable to Shasta since she was only twenty-two and her high school days seemed like eons ago.

The little crushes she'd had had come and gone, all except Nolt, but she had known he was never going to be a reality, so she put him out of her mind, although she supposed she judged every man she was with against him and always found them lacking.

"While I appreciate you coming, I'm much better and I feel like I can be by myself."

"Nolt talked about that. He was emphatic when he said he wanted me to stay."

"Why? I'm fine." She shrugged her shoulders. Sure, she still got tired, but she was doing much better.

"He said he promised the doctor that he wouldn't leave you home by yourself. But I feel like it goes deeper than that." Sadie lowered her head and looked at Shasta under her brows. "Is there something going on between you two?"

Shasta shook her head immediately. "Not at all. But he did see me when I was pretty sick. In fact, the doctor said I would have died if he hadn't taken me to the hospital. Maybe they say that to everyone, but..." She shrugged her shoulders. "Maybe he doesn't want all his hard work to go to waste."

"To have you die after he spent all the time taking care of you?" Sadie laughed.

"Yeah."

"I'm sure he doesn't." Sadie put her spoon down, her egg custard gone. "That was good. And I think whatever happened between you and Nolt, if anything, neither one of you is talking about it."

"There's nothing to talk about." Shasta raised her hands.

Sadie still didn't look like she believed her, but she changed the subject. "I don't know how much money the auction will bring in, of course, but I wanted to know if you had any jobs lined up?"

"Nothing. Although I'm still owed money from a job I did before I moved." She sighed, setting her spoon down, only one bite taken out of her egg custard. "I thought he was going to pay me, or I wouldn't have moved."

"Don't you demand money up front or something?" Sadie asked.

"I didn't feel like I could, since I'm new and everything. I mean, he'd seen samples of my work, and I know that's normally the way it's done, but...it was my first big job, and I was really excited about it."

"Understandable. Maybe he still will pay you. Have you reached out to him?"

"He's not answering my calls or my texts, but I sent him an email, and I haven't heard anything from that either."

"Did he know you were moving?"

Shasta nodded her head, frustrated with herself. She'd made some stupid mistakes. "He did. And maybe he took advantage of that. I feel dumb, on one hand, but on the other hand, doing that mural was really great experience for me. I... To be honest, when I started it, I wasn't sure whether I would be able to finish it or not."

"I think that's how everybody feels, isn't it? We doubt ourselves. Oftentimes, we doubt ourselves for no reason."

"I thought it was just me."

"I think that's everyone. It seems to be human nature."

"It's funny, because things that you know you can do, that you've done before, you look at them and you think how did I do that?"

"Exactly, and when you're asked to do it again, you think, 'Oh, I could never do that!'"

They laughed together, and Shasta had to admit what Sadie said made her feel better. Every time she got a job, she wondered if it was something she'd be able to do. And she felt guilty, like she was a fraud or fake or something, and how dare she insinuate that she would be able to draw or design or do whatever she was required to do. Even though she had her college degree behind her, she still felt...not real.

"I wish you were feeling better. It would have been fun for you to design the flyers for the auction. Everything is so last minute. I think they're just going up today." Sadie stood, reaching for Shasta's plate. "You don't want this?"

"Maybe I'll eat it later," Shasta said, knowing the refrigerator was already full of things she thought she might eat "later."

Sadie covered it with plastic wrap and set it in the refrigerator.

"I really love the idea of doing some kind of painting for the auction." Shasta racked her brain trying to think of something she could do that wouldn't be too taxing. And wouldn't take too long either, since she only had one day.

"Anything you could do would be good advertisement for you, because there are people coming from all around. Maybe something small?"

Sadie sat back down at the table, and they both were silent for a bit, thinking.

"You know, we're going to have signs marking each of the tables, and I think they've already been made. Just block lettering in black on a white background. Maybe I could bring those signs here, and you could spiff them up a little?"

"That's a great idea!" Shasta said. Excited. Not just because it would be a great advertisement for her, but also because she'd been sick for a week and hadn't painted anything. She longed to create. Even just a little.

Sadie pulled out her phone. "I'll text Nolt to see if he knows where they are, since he's organizing everything. Or at least heading it up. Flynn is really the one who knows how to keep things in line."

"He's the brother that keeps the books?"

"Yeah. And he definitely has a gift for organization." Sadie touched her laptop. "I wish I had it."

"You have other things."

"And so do you. I can't even draw."

"Sometimes it's a curse. Because you want to doodle on everything."

"I'll take your word for it. But I guess you're right, because I'm never tempted to doodle."

They chatted for a bit more, then Shasta excused herself to go lie down.

She had been thinking she might want to stay up until Nolt came with the signs. But she was exhausted and didn't want to push herself.

Every day, she could feel herself getting stronger. And she didn't want to have some kind of setback before the auction, something that might keep her from going.

Although, why it was so important to her to go, she wasn't quite sure. Maybe just to show up and thank everyone. Sweet Water had been so good to her. Nolt especially, and she felt like she owed them all. But she had no idea what she could do to pay them back.

She went to bed, dreaming of signs and flowers and men who played cards and laughed and hospital bills that were paid.

Chapter 8

Perseverance. Mainly just commitment. No matter what,
you are going to stick together.
- Joyce Marion from Florida (grew up in KY)

Nolt looked around the garage, barely recognizing it. He had organized everything and spent a lot of time cleaning, but Shasta, even though she hadn't set foot in the garage to his knowledge, had her touch everywhere, making things look pretty.

Beautiful.

From the signs hanging over every area of different auction items to the arrangements of flowers on the table, which would be auctioned off eventually, her touch was everywhere.

"We ran out of places to park people," Silas said, coming over and standing beside Nolt.

"The field is full?" Nolt turned with surprise and looked at his brother who nodded.

"It is. We actually had to ask Mr. Richardson if it was okay if we started parking people across the road. Of course he gave us permission, but it's unexpected."

"I'll say." He crossed his arms over his chest and surveyed the room again, looking for something that was out of place, something that needed to be done. They'd worked hard to not have to do things at the last minute, but now it felt odd to be idle, to not be working at something. "I can't believe for such a short notice, it's so well attended."

"I think it pulls at people's heartstrings. And especially because they know she was working hard to take care of herself. Probably being a foster child didn't hurt."

"She was a foster kid?" Nolt asked, unable to contain his surprise.

"You spent more than a week with her and you didn't know that?" Silas returned, shoving his hands in his pockets and looking around. Nolt could tell the very second his eyes landed on his wife, because they brightened, and he smiled.

Nolt's gaze followed his over to where Gladys stood, chatting with some other ladies as they arranged pies on a table. His brother's expression—of admiration and love—warmed his own heart, but it also gave him a discontented twist in his chest.

Anytime he saw a couple happy together, it made him glad. Especially his own family. Because so many couples didn't make it.

But it always reminded him of Alana and how she would never be his. Or maybe it was just the idea that she had chosen someone else, and he was destined to be alone.

"Didn't you guys talk at all? Couldn't you get your measly mouth open and entertain her just a little?"

Nolt shook his head and looked at his brother. "We talked."

"Obviously not about important stuff if you didn't know she was a foster child."

"Maybe she didn't want to talk about her family." That was the reason. He'd asked twice, not probing questions but just general ones, and she brushed him off. It annoyed him a little, made him wonder what was wrong with him that she obviously was talking to other people but didn't want to talk to him.

Had he been too intimidating?

He remembered them laughing together as they played games and lying behind her in the bed, warming her up. Standing in the kitchen warming up food for her and trying to think of outrageous bribes to get her to eat it.

Surely after all the time they'd spent together, she trusted him.

"I think people just like to have an excuse to get together," he said, maybe trying to shift the subject a little. He didn't know why she hadn't told him.

"Yeah. That's probably it." Silas's voice was flat, and he might as well have rolled his eyes and said "there's no way."

Both of them let it go. A big part of being the oldest of seven kids was letting things go.

"There's a couple of really nice quarter horses out there."

"Horses?" Nolt asked, surprised again. It seemed like tonight was destined to be a night of surprises.

"Yeah. Surprised me too." Silas jerked his head. "We've got a little time. Want to come on out and see them?"

Nolt didn't want to get distracted and forget that tonight wasn't about him. That he was supposed to be supervising things and not being entertained. But while trucks were his livelihood, he'd always loved horses. And couldn't resist following his brother to the door.

They nodded at people in greeting, but the crowd seemed to part for them, like folks knew that they needed to make sure everything was going smoothly, and no one stopped them to chat.

Both of the big garage doors on the end were open, and once they stepped out, it was easy to see the two beautiful palominos standing in the middle of a crowd of people, their manes blowing along with their tails in the slight afternoon breeze.

They were gorgeous, with the large hindquarters that marked good breeding on a quarter horse, and looked well cared for as their coats glistened in the sun.

"Wow. I hope they get what those are worth."

"I don't think they would have brought them if they hadn't thought they would. But I've seen five or six horse people here. I'm assuming they came because they heard about them." Silas nodded his head at the pair.

As Nolt looked back over, his eyes caught on a gleam of honey-colored hair. Familiar.

Shasta stood by herself in the parking lot, her arms around what looked like tablecloths or some type of material, and he would guess she had been bringing them from someone's car. But her attention had gotten caught by the horses, and she'd stopped.

He watched as she admired them, just staring with a little smile tilting her lips up.

What was going through her head? They'd talked a little bit about coveting, and they'd talk a lot more about the fact that she didn't have any money.

She wasn't thinking about buying horses, but it was pretty obvious she admired them.

Admiration didn't necessarily have to translate into ownership, and some people were perfectly content to look at things and never buy.

But he could imagine Shasta, with her love of beauty and her special talent to make the things around her look gorgeous, taking an early morning ride, watching the sunrise, memorizing the colors and how they flowed in her brain, and having those same colors come out of her fingers later.

Something about the girl and the horses stirred his soul, and from somewhere, the thought came, *if she were mine, we'd have horses.*

It took him about three seconds to realize what he just thought, and he shifted his gaze away, frustrated with himself.

Shasta was his baby sister's friend. She was too young for him, and he felt like he was not being faithful to Alana by thinking about Shasta.

Never mind that Alana had walked out of his life years ago; he'd just gotten stuck, and he continued to be faithful, whether or not the people around him were.

It was just how he was.

"Hey. I see my wife waving at me, she must need something." Silas jogged off, after Nolt jerked his head.

He should be helping with something too.

"She's pretty," a voice said beside him, and he looked over to see his dad.

"They're beautiful," he said, wondering why his dad said "she," like there was only one horse.

His dad's eyes crinkled, and he shook his head. "You weren't looking at the horses."

Nolt started to furrow his brows and act like he didn't know what his dad was talking about, but that was just pretending, which was almost the same as lying.

And it was his dad.

"She is pretty," he acknowledged, not allowing his voice to curl around the words like he wanted it to. He said it matter-of-factly. Like she didn't mean anything to him. Because she really didn't. Only as a friend.

"That's not the way you were looking at her." His dad raised his brows and stood his ground, and Nolt felt like he was standing in front of his dad's desk as an adolescent in trouble for something.

He lifted his shoulder. "I don't know how I was looking at her, but she's not Alana, and I guess I'm just not interested."

"Still stuck on Alana?" his dad said, like it wasn't a surprise.

Nolt figured it wasn't, not to his family anyway. They knew he had perseverance and determination, some might term it stubbornness, and once he started on a path, he didn't deviate. He stuck. That was what he did. He was faithful and consistent.

"You know what they say, some men only fall in love once."

It felt a little uncomfortable to talk about falling in love. The mushy, gushy feelings he wished he didn't have, but he didn't want his dad getting any ideas about Shasta and him.

He didn't want anyone getting any ideas about that.

His bet paid off, because his dad didn't say anything, just crossed his arms over his chest and seemed to look between Shasta and the horses.

"You know your farm could use some animals."

While Nolt was relieved his dad had chosen a different subject, one that didn't involve Shasta, Nolt shook his head.

"I don't have time. I love them, but right now, I don't have anything tying me down, and I can go wherever the company needs me."

"Well, just saying, since your girl over there seems to really like them, and having a wife around the place eases the burden a little for you, you could do something nice for her."

Nolt crossed his arms over his chest and tried not to laugh. At himself. Because he thought he'd gotten his dad to change the subject.

He hadn't.

"I don't think I'll ever have a wife."

He was frustrated with himself because what he meant to say was, "I will never have a wife." It's what he would have said last month or last year. But... The belief had softened in his mind, and he figured he knew exactly who his dad would blame for it anyway.

"I'd like to take you out for breakfast tomorrow," his dad said thoughtfully.

Nolt's brows raised. It wasn't that he never ate with his dad. They did it often when they traveled for their company, whether they were fixing a truck on the road or going to look at grain still standing in the field.

The odd thing was that they were doing it without having any business to take care of as well. A trip just to go out to eat was a luxury they didn't often indulge in.

"I'd like that."

"We'll probably be tired from cleaning up here tonight, so doesn't have to be early. Ten or so."

Nolt couldn't help but think that his dad was up to something, but he wasn't sure what it could be, and he supposed if it involved food, he'd be in for it.

And if the boss wanted to take him out to eat, he wasn't going to be in trouble for not doing his job.

"Sounds good," he said, watching despite himself as Shasta moved from her position where she'd been watching the horses and started walking toward the garage.

Her movements were slow, and as Nolt watched her, he could see the pinching of her eyes and the shadows under them.

She'd barely been out of bed two days ago, and now she was walking around carrying stuff.

He wanted to tell her to go sit down. Wanted to actually take the stuff out of her hands, carry it for her, and lead her to a chair. But he'd just argued with his dad that she didn't mean anything to him, and for him to do what he wanted to, it would make his words look empty.

So, when she slowed down as she walked in front of them, looking at them with a smile on her face, he nodded at her, then so she wouldn't be tempted to stop and talk, he deliberately lifted his eyes from her and looked back at the horses.

His dad murmured, "Let me help you with that," and Shasta thanked him as his dad took the stuff from her arms, and they walked into the garage together. Leaving Nolt standing there with his arms crossed, feeling like a jerk.

He should have offered to help. He shouldn't be so worried about what the rest of the world was thinking.

Maybe, rather than sitting around pining for the girl he thought God had meant for him years ago, and instead of thinking he knew what was best for his life, maybe he should just ask the Lord and see what God had to say about it.

As soon as the thought came to him, he knew it was the right one.

He'd been the one going around insisting that Shasta wasn't for him, she was too young, she was not Alana, he didn't want to get married.

Maybe he should stop being so arrogant and be a little bit more humble.

Chapter 9

Fun - have fun and laugh together.
Joyce Marion from Florida (grew up in KY)

L aughter filled the garage as Shasta stood on the makeshift platform, exhausted but happy.

She'd just thanked everyone for coming and for every donation and just expressed her gratitude that everyone had been so supportive and sweet to her.

Sadie had told everyone that she was still recovering and might not make it through the entire evening, that she might need to rest and to take it easy since she still tired so easily.

She appreciated Sadie beside her and squeezed her waist as they walked off the platform together.

Sadie squeezed her back. "You were awesome."

She didn't know about that. Getting up in front of people wasn't something she was good at, like most of the rest of the world's population, but she had really wanted to. Just because the town of Sweet Water had been so kind and amazing to her. She wished there was something she could do to give back a little.

The same way she wished she could pay Nolt back, since he was the one who really spearheaded everything.

She'd mentioned him in her comments, but just in passing. He'd seemed to go out of his way to avoid her today and hadn't exactly looked happy to see her the one time she passed him.

In fact, his dad was the one who had come over to help her, while Nolt had turned away.

"How are you holding up?" Sadie asked as they smiled at people, making their way toward the back of the garage. The auctioneer had his mic up front, and they were going to start with the craft items, household goods, and garage donations before they moved to the baskets of food, then took a break for supper.

"I'm doing okay. I know I'm not going to make it the whole way through. Maybe I'll just go find a quiet spot to sit down for a little bit."

"You can use my office. I know we talked about it, and I think Nolt actually put a lawn chair in there, one of those ones that you can lie down on," Sadie said. "You can lock the door and pull the blinds, and no one will be able to see in."

"You've all been so thoughtful," Shasta said, her chest feeling full and good and the words getting stuck in her throat.

The whole time she'd been roommates with Sadie, she'd known Sadie was a wonderful person. Considerate and sweet. She had changed a bit since they graduated, in fact, had maybe gotten better.

Shasta rested for a bit but truly hated to miss anything. It was a night that people had come together to help her, and her limbs felt like dead weights, and it seemed to take a lot of energy to smile, let alone talk, but she didn't want to miss a minute.

She came out just as they finished up selling the household stuff and began selling one of the bouquets of wildflowers that Sadie had brought her earlier that morning to arrange. Shasta had made the bouquets, and Sadie had set them on the tables.

She stood in the back, looking over the heads of the people, most of them listening to the auction, some of them chatting, some of them moving along the tables of food, picking up a cookie, or admiring the paintings she had done for each section of auction items.

Soon the crowd would eat, then move outside as they auctioned off the larger items.

There would be dancing afterward, and Sadie had said people might end up staying until quite late.

Back in Nebraska, where she grew up, people were just as friendly and kind, but she'd never been to anything quite like this. If this is what the people in Sweet Water did for fun, she wished she could stay.

The bidding had slowed down, and there were just two or three people the auctioneer moved between.

She couldn't believe the bid was up to fifty dollars for a vase that Sadie had found in their house and an arrangement of wildflowers.

Sadie had been so complimentary over them though, saying that not everyone could arrange flowers like that and that they would not only have them to decorate the tables, but they'd have to auction them off.

Shasta had been leery, but she would have to admit to her friend she was right.

The bid had gone over seventy-five dollars, and Shasta looked around, trying to figure out who was still bidding.

The man who had brought the horses in, Ford Hanson from outside Sweet Water, raised his hand for eighty dollars.

"I've got eighty. Who will give me eighty-five? Eighty-five?"

He droned on and on, and Shasta's gaze scanned the crowd again, trying to figure out who the other bidder was.

It only took a couple of seconds before she saw a young boy, maybe twelve years old, waving his hand. No wonder the auctioneer smiled every other time he got a bid.

"All right. I got ninety. Who will give me ninety-five? Ninety-five?"

"Nolt gave that little fella a hundred dollars and told him to bid it all on flowers for his mom."

Shasta looked over at the woman behind the voice.

Mrs. Baldwin. Marigold's mother, although she also had five other children, if Shasta remembered correctly.

"That's so sweet," she said, scanning the crowd again and looking for Nolt.

He stood in the back, clear over at the other corner, and she would have expected him to be watching the boy, but as she looked, his eyes were on her.

"I heard you arranged those flowers yourself," Mrs. Baldwin said.

She nodded. "One of my foster parents owned a floral shop. That was probably the best place I stayed. I just loved helping there."

The woman had gotten sick and hadn't been able to keep her, and the state had placed her in a different home.

Sometimes she wondered what happened to them, but she'd been with so many—five or six—different homes, she lost track of addresses and names.

"You have a real talent. If the price isn't quite that high later, I might bid on some myself. They look like wildflowers from along the road, only you arrange them so beautifully, they're a work of art."

"They *are* wildflowers from along the road. I told Sadie I'd decorate the tables if she would get me the flowers."

"Must be awesome to have that kind of talent. To create something out of just a few little odds and ends." Mrs. Baldwin, with her dark tan and graying hair and shrewd eyes, could be a little intimidating.

From what Sadie had told her, her husband had died more than a decade ago and had left her to raise her six children alone as well as run the auction barn in town.

Mrs. Baldwin had not only risen to the challenge but, between her and her oldest son, had made the auction barn the most successful one in the state.

While her smile was still tender, there wasn't much softness about her. The compliments that she gave were no-nonsense and sincere.

"Thank you. I guess it's just one of those things that God gives us, and..." She thought of some of the things that she and Nolt had talked about while she'd been recovering.

"And you just have to use what God has given you and love your work," Mrs. Baldwin said.

"That's right. Because it's all His anyway."

"You do an excellent job of using all God has given you and shining His glory back on Him." Mrs. Baldwin's gaze was benevolent, but then something seemed to catch her eye, and she looked up.

Mr. Powers walked toward them, and for the first time, Mrs. Baldwin seemed tense and not relaxed.

"It was nice chatting with you," Mrs. Baldwin said, not sounding rushed or hurried but somehow seeming that way.

They murmured goodbye to each other, and Mrs. Baldwin strode away.

When Shasta looked back, Mr. Powers had stopped where he was, right in the middle of the floor, and turned back toward the auction, where the young boy had won the flowers for one hundred dollars even.

The whole crowd erupted into applause as the boy proudly went up, handed over his money, and took the flowers.

He walked directly to his mom, whom Shasta recognized as Peyton, a single mom who had recently opened the bookstore and whom Shasta rented her apartment from.

She had wondered how they split the small apartment, which was exactly the same size as Shasta's, on the other side of the bookstore.

Still, Peyton beamed as her son handed her the flowers and kissed her cheek.

The crowd's applause grew even louder as Peyton's cheeks got red, and she hugged her boy while holding the flowers with one hand.

Shasta couldn't keep herself from grinning. The whole town must have been involved, because Nolt might have given him the money, but the fact that the bidding stopped right at the amount that he had offered told her that Ford, the other bidder, had known exactly how much money the kid had and helped him spend every penny of it.

She loved that spirit of the town, the one that worked behind the scenes to bring smiles to people's faces, and she loved even more that the flowers that she had arranged were part of that.

Her suspicions were confirmed as she glanced over at Nolt, who was not looking at her but who met the gaze of someone across the room. When Shasta looked over, it was Ford, his scarred face lifting in a grin, his one eye hidden by an eyepatch, the other one twinkling.

Shasta felt like she was witnessing a private moment as the two men shared a smile, then Ford's arm squeezed around his wife, who was one of the most beautiful women Shasta had ever seen, and she looked up adoringly at her husband.

Lord, please help me find enough work here so that I can afford to stay. What an amazing town. What amazing people. It's inspiring how they look out for each other, even me, who doesn't even really belong, and how they lift each other up.

Sweet Water was a special place indeed, and she hoped with all her heart that God would answer her prayer and allow her to stay.

Chapter 10

Both being believers and good communication.
- Mary Garback from Ridgecrest, CA

T he auction was over.

The Mustang had sold for more than Nolt had imagined, and the horses for almost as much, although they hadn't gone together, with one going to New York, and one had been bought by an online bidder and was headed to Texas.

He didn't know how much Shasta's medical bills were going to be, but tonight they were able to make a huge dent in them, if not cover them completely.

It felt good. Worth the long hours and stressful week. Worth all the cleaning and organizing he had done.

Everything was worth it to see Shasta's smile grow bigger and bigger all night.

Of course, she had looked more tired each time he'd seen her as well.

He mentioned to Sadie twice that Sadie should suggest she rest.

He was on his way to suggest it again. As far as he knew, Shasta had only disappeared into Sadie's office once, and she'd been interacting with people ever since.

Right now, she stood in a group that included Boone and Roxane from the Sweet Water Ranch, along with Lark and her brother, whom everyone called Preacher, with his family.

As happy as he was that she was getting to know the Stryker family, she was overdoing it, and he couldn't deny he was concerned.

"Sadie, you need to tell Shasta she needs to go lie down for a bit. Or send her home." He spoke in Sadie's ear as she bent over the dessert table, grabbing another cookie.

She jumped, then put a hand to her heart. "Don't do that. You scared me."

"There's two hundred people in this building. You can't tell me you're surprised to hear one of them talking."

"Not two inches from my ear!" Sadie said, her eyes big, then she ruined the whole effect by taking a bite of her cookie. "I have to self-medicate," she said with a mouthful.

"Self-medicate on your way over to Shasta, and tell her she's overdone it and she needs to at least sit down, if not go somewhere and lie down."

Sadie stared at him, her eyes big and blinking, while she chewed her cookie in big chopping bites.

Swallowing, she opened her mouth, put one hand on her hip, and leveled a glare at him. "You tell her."

She smirked, narrowed her eyes for a second, swiped another cookie off of the table, and walked in the exact opposite direction of where Shasta was standing.

Nolt figured it probably served him right, but he was still annoyed at his sister.

Shasta was going to end up back in the hospital if she didn't settle down and take care of herself.

As he stood there thinking about it, all the nights he'd spent sitting up listening to her breathe, making her drink, wheedling her to eat, time in the hospital, and how he found her almost dead on the floor flowed through his head, and anger, and maybe determination, that stubbornness he seemed to be born with, built up inside of him, until he decided that he had every right in the world to walk over there and tell her that he didn't want her undoing all of the hard work he'd put into making sure she got better.

Maybe that is not the most caring way to approach the subject.

He supposed that was his inner feminine side coming out. He hadn't been in touch with that side much during his life, but it seemed to be making an appearance more, since he'd spent time with Shasta.

He was already on his way over though, and Shasta had looked up to see him coming, so he didn't veer away.

He did try to modulate his steps so he wasn't stomping.

He had timed his approach perfectly, since the Strykers had moved away, and he was able to take a hold of Shasta's arm and say to the two people who remained, "Do you mind if I borrow Shasta for a moment, please?"

It was a question, but he said it as a statement, like it was a given that he was taking her.

She went with him without protesting, which surprised him. He kind of thought she would argue or at least be offended that he wasn't giving her a choice, since he didn't exactly ask her if she wanted to come.

He appreciated that. Though, maybe he was being a little high-handed, but if men were expected to be okay when women were emotional, maybe it was okay for men to expect women to understand when they got bossy and commanding, as that was their nature just as much as being emotional was for women.

Nolt was pretty happy with his argument in his head when Shasta dug in her feet and pulled him to a stop.

"Where are you taking me?" she asked, her face set in a mulish look as she pulled her arm away and crossed it over her chest.

"I wanted to talk to you."

"Then, it would be polite for you to say, 'Shasta, do you have a moment? I'd like to talk to you.'"

All his fine words about men being commanding and putting up with women being emotional, so women should do the same, flew out of his head.

His mouth opened and closed twice before he decided that probably wasn't a smart idea anyway.

"I'm sorry." He lifted his chin a little and took a breath, not bothering to hide it, letting her know almost in a teasing way that he was doing something hard. "Shasta. I'd like to speak with you for a moment. Would you mind walking outside with me?"

She smiled, which he considered a win, since that's what he was going for. Humor.

"I'm tired," she said, rather than agreeing.

"That's what I wanted to talk to you about. Do I need to carry you out?" he asked, moving a little closer to her and bending over just a little. She knew he could, and he would too.

"No. I can walk." She might have moved back, but it was obvious that she was completely exhausted.

Her shoulders slumped, and her face seemed drawn. The big smile she'd been wearing just a few minutes ago was completely gone, and while he figured it meant she trusted him since she allowed him to see exactly how tired she was, it worried him too.

"Come on. We can still hear the music outside a little, and we can find a place to sit down."

She nodded, agreeing easier than he thought she would and allowing him to put his arm around her waist as he led her outside.

Chapter 11

Respect, and having the same goals.
- Dalila Felaco from Venezuela, living in the United King-
dom

T hey stepped out into the darkness, a long shaft of light illu-
minating the parking lot before Nolt closed the door and it
disappeared.

He had his arm around Shasta, and she seemed to lean against
him as they stepped out into the cool night.

He pulled her closer, and he told himself it was because he was
supporting her and had nothing to do with how good she felt or the
sigh he barely heard her breathe out or the release of the nagging
feeling of discontent that had been plaguing him all evening.

"We can sit in the chairs back here." He moved in the direction of
the lawn chairs which sat behind the garage. He and his brothers
used them at lunchtime sometimes.

"Can we stay here?" Shasta asked softly. "We can hear the music
and see the moon."

"We can, but you look like you're going to collapse. That was the
reason we came out."

She moved, turning against him, until her front was pressed to
his and her arms wound around his neck. Without thinking, his
arms moved to support her, and he held her close.

"Dance with me. Then we won't have to think about sitting down, and we can just enjoy the night together. I promise, I'll lay my head on your chest and it will be just like resting."

Maybe she was teasing him a little. He wasn't really in the mood to smile. He wanted this to be serious, wanted it to be real.

Except he didn't. He didn't want it to end.

Still, he slid one hand around the back of her head and pressed gently. She laid her head on his chest, her arms holding onto his waist, and he swayed gently with her. The breeze whispering against them, the music soft and low, muted from inside, a few indistinct voices murmuring in the field across the road as people walked to their cars. The satisfaction of an evening of fun and fellowship, good times and a good cause, swelled around, building contentment and peace deep in his soul.

"I wanted to thank you again for tonight."

"That's what friends do."

"No. This is far beyond what normal friends do. Thank you."

"Friends rest when they're exhausted and just recovering from being so sick they almost died."

He didn't want to talk about what he had done or how she was grateful. It made him uncomfortable. He didn't do it for the accolades, although he had done it because he cared and her words made his heart smile. He liked that she noticed and was grateful. He just...didn't know how to respond. "You're welcome" made it sound like he was acknowledging that there was something good in him, and he couldn't help but feel that there really wasn't.

Her body moved against his, and he was amazed that it fit so perfectly. Wished they could just sway there all night, holding each other, listening to the music, and having just the stars and the moon for witnesses. The soft breeze as company. The closeness of just the two of them in the universe, small yet perfect and somehow bigger, more, together.

"I haven't gotten any bills from the hospital."

"We've been talking to the bank, and they've agreed to keep this money in a special account for you. Everything that comes in will be there, and we can make some decisions on how we pay those bills. Every cent left over is yours."

"Unless I don't need it."

"You keep what's left."

"I can't do that."

"That's what tonight was for. You."

"To pay my hospital bills. Not to line my pockets."

"You're not lining your pockets. You'll have a little money jingling around so you're not pressed for time while you look for work."

She was quiet for a bit, and he figured she saw the wisdom in what he said. He suspected she would have a little extra, but he could be wrong. He didn't want to get her hopes up if not. And they wouldn't know until the hospital sent the bills, which sometimes could take a while.

"Nolt?"

"Hmm?" he said, only half paying attention. He rested the side of his jaw on the top of her head and looked at the stars and the horizon, thinking what a beautiful land they lived in, and how content he was, and he didn't really want to be jolted out of his contemplation with words or talking.

"I know you took care of me because of your sister."

"Partly," he murmured, feeling the brush of his lips against her hair and wondering what it would be like to kiss her.

Funny how darkness and music and the right girl in his arms could make a man think about kissing. Think about kissing to the point where he didn't want to think about anything else.

"And I know you had this tonight just because that's the kind of person you are."

He didn't want to take credit where it wasn't due, and that definitely wasn't due, but he didn't want to argue.

So he just said, "Not always."

She swallowed and took a deep breath, although her head never left his chest.

He felt warm and happy in all the right places and breathed in deeply, letting the scent of berries and vanilla permeate his brain. Anytime he smelled that in the future, he'd remember this night.

"I know Sadie is your sister. And you think of her as your baby sister. You kind of see me in the same light since we're the same age."

For the first time since Shasta started talking, he felt a sense of foreboding. He pushed it aside. He didn't want to ruin tonight.

"I kind of feel like maybe there might be something more there, because while all the things that you've been doing have been nice, and there are reasons for you to do them, I feel like there might be something more."

She stopped swaying with him and pulled back a bit, her arms dropping to hold either side of his waist as she looked up into his eyes.

The moonlight glistened on her face, causing her eyes to sparkle, as her hair blew gently in the breeze.

He missed feeling her under his jaw and the scent of her under his nose. He wanted her back, closer. But he waited.

"I want there to be more, Nolt. I like you as a friend, for sure, but...I think I'm falling for you."

Her words took a few seconds to make their way into the happy fog that had gathered in his brain. And by then, she was reaching up, standing on her tiptoes, and tugging his head down.

He wanted to jerk back and tell her that she was wrong. She wasn't falling for him. This wasn't more than friends. This was just him helping her out.

But then her lips touched his, and he forgot about the words he wanted to say, and the fact that she was so much younger than him, and couldn't have told anyone the name of the girl that he was supposed to be pining for, as Shasta pressed into him, her lips moving over his, her hands in his hair, her body almost close enough. Before he realized it, he was kissing her back, moving her closer, feeling the heat shoot through his veins as she moved under his hands and her mouth moved under his, deepening their kiss, pulling him into her despite his thumping heart and swimming head and lungs that screamed for air.

She sighed a little against his lips, and he realized the sound that answered her was his own, deeper sigh, although he didn't recognize it.

Maybe they would have stood there and kissed all night, maybe he would never have found his head and had his rational thinking return and remembered all the things that he wanted to say and all the reasons he had for why he didn't want to do this, but the door opened and light spilled out.

He jerked back, almost not catching her as she stumbled forward, falling into his chest.

He set his hands on her shoulders as the door closed again, although he never looked toward it. He steadied her, his arms stretched out, holding her just that far away from him, while he caught his breath and tried to find the words he needed to say.

Needed to, but didn't want to.

He fought back, because he wasn't going to allow one kiss to change the things he'd believed for the last two decades.

"No." He gulped a breath and made his voice level. Cool. Un-emotional. Completely opposite from the kiss they'd just shared, which had been so beautifully full of warm, sweet emotions he wasn't sure he'd ever recover. "I'm sorry about that. That shouldn't have happened. And you're not right. You're not falling for me. You're just happy to be alive and grateful that I helped you. You can consider that kiss payment in full."

He dropped his hands, making sure she was steady on her feet before he backed even further away. "I'm going to get Sadie and tell her you're ready to go home."

He turned quickly, striding for the door, already feeling terrible because he knew his words had most definitely not been what she wanted to hear, but he knew they were the right ones.

She wasn't falling in love with him. And he, most certainly, was not falling for her.

Chapter 12

Decide to stick with it. Work thru problems & don't give up.
PRAY a lot.
- Cindy Jones

S hasta lay in bed, lethargic.

It must have been almost noon, considering the glow and the angle of the sun coming in the window, but she felt too tired to move.

Last night had been a dream. So beautiful. The town, the people, the love they showed her, the friendly get-together and casual enjoyment of each other, the beautiful generosity, good food, and...she'd been so sure Nolt had been looking at her all evening.

Every time she looked at him, she caught him staring straight at her.

The conspiracy that he had with Ford, and the twelve-year-old buying flowers for his mom, and the way Nolt had cared for her, and the times Sadie had come over and whispered in her ear that Nolt was nagging her again about making Shasta rest...

All of that had worked together in her heart, making her fall even more for the quiet cowboy and convincing herself that he felt the same way about her.

She groaned, burying her face in her pillow and wondering why she couldn't cry.

Last night, she figured she'd been too tired, and Sadie hadn't questioned her on the way home when she'd been quiet and still.

Surely Sadie had chalked that up to exhaustion, but Shasta felt heartbroken.

Her chest hurt. A dull ache, with sharp pains that shot out every few minutes. Reminding her that she'd been rejected.

It was one thing to harbor a dream, sweet and safe and comfortable, close to her heart, nurturing it and getting it out every once in a while to smile at and think about.

It was another thing to have that dream be brutally shattered into so many tiny little pieces there was no way she could ever pick them up and put them back together.

That dream was gone.

Which didn't mean she no longer had feelings for Nolt, because she did. He was a good man, and she admired him. And she hadn't been lying when she said she was falling for him. Her feelings were definitely strong, although she wasn't sure whether she would term them love.

But he didn't return them, and she had to figure something else out. He said all along that he didn't, so he'd never led her on with words. She'd just read too much in his actions. Put things in them that weren't there, because she wanted them to be. Not because they were.

Part of getting through it would be putting distance between herself and him. Maybe God hadn't given her any more work in Sweet Water because he didn't want her to stay in Sweet Water, as much as she wanted to.

Of course, she had gotten some leads last night, people asking for her number and email and saying they would contact her.

Nothing solid. Maybe they were just talking.

Pounding on her door startled her, jerking her fully awake, and had her sitting up before she realized what it was.

"Come in! The door's open."

A second of silence ensued before the knob turned, and Sadie walked in.

She was still dressed in her church clothes, and Shasta felt a twinge of guilt for not getting up and going to the services.

She still didn't feel like getting out of bed. Whether that was because she was exhausted from last night or depressed because of Nolt, she wasn't sure.

"Goodness, it's one o'clock in the afternoon!" Sadie said, breezing in and setting her Bible on Shasta's secondhand dresser before pulling up the seat beside the bed. "I heard all about the people who are emailing you. What do you think?"

"What do you mean what do I think?" Shasta said, her brows drawing together as she tried to remember where she'd dropped her phone last night before she dropped herself in bed.

Sadie got up from the chair and went over to the dresser, grabbing her phone and bringing it back.

"Do you mind if I stay while you look?" she asked, an excited smile hovering around her mouth.

That's the kind of friend Sadie had always been, happy for her when things went well.

She'd had plenty of friends over the years who begrudged her success, or who just disappeared when things were going well, or worse, who talked about her behind her back because of jealousy and spite.

Sadie had never been like that. That was part of what made her a really great friend.

Her excitement had Shasta smiling as she glanced at her screen and saw so many email and text notifications, she couldn't tell how many there were.

She unlocked it and pulled up her email. Thirty new messages. Not quite that many texts.

She started opening them, smiling, as she read snippets to Sadie. "This person wants me to paint designs on their grandmother's china."

She lifted horrified eyes to Sadie. She didn't want to be responsible for someone's grandmother's china.

"It probably came out here on a Conestoga wagon," Sadie dead-panned.

"And this one wants to know about painting a mural in their son's nursery. And this one..." Shasta's voice drifted off as she read the email. This one was serious. Not that the other ones weren't, but this one was worth a lot of money.

"What? What is it?" Sadie said, coming around and trying to read over Shasta's shoulder as she leaned up in bed.

"This person... I think he's the guy from New York who bought the horse last night."

"Those horses were gorgeous," Sadie said, almost absentmind-edly, because then she said quickly, "Go on!"

"Let me read it: Dear Shasta, it was a pleasure to speak with you last night blah blah blah..." She skimmed down to where the information started in earnest. "One of my hobbies is restoring old barns. In my mind as I've done this, I'd imagine that part of the restoration process would involve painting murals on the barns. Until yesterday, I didn't have a clear idea in my head of exactly what I wanted. But when I saw your artwork, I knew you were the one I wanted to do my barns. I have ten, and I usually add two or three every year." She skimmed down, although she almost shouted when the letter mentioned the amount of money he said she would earn per barn. Not including supplies.

Sadie squealed, and they ended up hugging each other on the bed, laughing and saying things like, "I can't believe it!" and "This is unreal!" and "This is a dream job!"

They giggled, like teenagers talking about their crushes, until Sadie sat up suddenly and said, "Does he have a time frame?"

Shasta blinked and pushed up slowly, still not feeling quite as energetic as she'd like to.

She grabbed her phone and scanned down the email.

"He wants me to start as soon as I can." Her voice was more subdued, maybe even sad. Because, although the money was more than she had imagined, it meant she'd be in New York.

"That's great!" Sadie said, although her tone wasn't nearly as excited as it had been either. "You'll be a New Yorker." She wiggled her brows.

"I think this is upstate New York... Yeah. He says the Finger Lakes region. That's like another world from New York City."

"Good. I wouldn't want you to get all snobby on me," Sadie said, bumping Shasta with her shoulder to let her know she was joking.

"I wouldn't want to go to the city." She didn't add that she would if she had to, if that was the only way she could make money.

"Okay," Sadie said after taking a deep breath and looking at Shasta. "You love the idea of making all that money, and I think you love the idea of the barn mural, but it's New York." She pointed at the phone. "Want to see if the other offers you have would be enough for you to make enough money to stay here or to go wherever you wanted to go?"

Somehow that question made Shasta remember that if she wanted to get over Nolt, she needed to get away from him. Maybe this was God's way of providing an opportunity out.

"I'm feeling a little overwhelmed. I think I'm going to have to think about this." She lifted eyes to Sadie, who immediately seemed like she understood.

"You had some big days. And you're still getting better. I didn't mean to come in here and rock your world. I'm just happy for you." Her face fell as her hand slipped off of Shasta's arm. "But it kinda makes me sad too. The idea of you leaving."

"Yeah. Me too. Last night was one of the best nights of my life. And not because it was about me, but just because of all the people in this town and the kind things they did..." Her voice trailed off as she realized that it really was the best night of her life, but it didn't end well.

She wouldn't term it the worst night of her life though, although it was definitely the hardest rejection she'd ever had.

"You know, that guy from New York? I thought he kinda had a crush on you. The way he was talking about you and everything. It doesn't really surprise me that he sent you an email today. What does surprise me is that he didn't ask you out too." Sadie grinned as she hopped off the bed. "I could have told him that you're so stuck on Nolt you wouldn't even look at him, but it was fun to see how besotted with you he was."

Thankfully Sadie turned to go, walking to the dresser and picking up her Bible, which gave Shasta time to rearrange her face.

She hadn't even noticed the guy from New York. Barely. He'd been rattling on about barns and horses and things he did in his spare time, and he made some jokes that if Nolt had said them, she'd have been laughing just because it was Nolt, but because it was some dude she didn't even know, they felt lame.

"You know, I wouldn't mind if some guy got besotted like that with me," Sadie said, and Shasta figured she was only half joking.

"Maybe men just are really attracted to lethargic women who look like they can barely stand on their own two feet and are going to fall over at any second," she said, giving her friend an ironic grin.

"Maybe I'll try that next time." She was being sarcastic, but then she sobered. "Maybe men don't want women who can take care of themselves."

"I think you just have to find the right man. Some women want a man to take care of them."

"That sounds good in theory, but in practice, I don't really like being told what to do."

"You can't have it all, right?"

They grinned at each other, and then Sadie came back over, putting a hand on Shasta's head and smoothing her hair back.

"I'm sorry. I didn't mean to come wake you up. Yesterday was a big day, and you probably need all the rest you can get. Plus, now you have a big decision to make, and it's a good one. I mean, everywhere you look, somebody wants to pay you for painting, and that's like a dream come true, right?"

Shasta nodded. It was funny how the work was bittersweet, because of Nolt's rejection.

"Sadie?"

"Yeah," Sadie said, giving Shasta's hair one last pat then wrapping her arms around her waist while standing beside the bed with a questioning look on her face.

"I don't want to be stuck on Nolt."

Sadie's head tilted. "Why not? He's stuck on you." She started to turn to go.

"No. He's not. I...asked him last night to be more than friends, and he was pretty quick to reject me."

She tried not to let her voice show the depth of emotion she felt over that. She didn't want sympathy. She had enough sympathy to last her decades. But she couldn't think of the kiss without feeling like she wanted him to hold her forever.

She wanted more.

"Nolt's tough. He's really closed off. He was rejected once, and it really affected him. I think he fancies himself still in love with her, but he doesn't even know her." Sadie lifted her phone up. "I need to get going. Flynn is waiting on me so they can eat lunch."

Shasta nodded and returned Sadie's hug, then watched as she walked out.

Shasta had been so sure that she knew how Nolt was feeling. Just like Sadie was.

She thought she'd be safe to say what she had. She thought she was just saying what both of them wanted. Especially while he held her in the moonlight.

Maybe that was why moonlight was so dangerous. It started putting thoughts in her head that weren't true. Started making her think people felt things for her they didn't. Started making her think that she could take chances and do crazy things that were going to end up hurting. A lot.

And then there was that kiss.

It had been magical. Beautiful. And yet, the memory was sour because she thought Nolt had been kissing her back, but he couldn't have been. With that knowledge, in her mind the kiss degenerated into something that just caused embarrassment.

The most wonderful, amazing thing that ever happened to her, and to him, it was just trash.

Now it was something she wished she could forget. Because it embarrassed her. She'd kissed a man who hadn't wanted her to and who had thoroughly rejected her after she was done.

It didn't get much worse than that.

Looking at her phone once more, it was hard to dredge up excitement about the jobs she'd been offered, when all she wanted to do was lie around and be depressed.

Grabbing her phone, she set an alarm for two hours.

She'd give herself two hours to mope and feel bad, and then she was going to get on her phone, read all the messages, lay them all out before the Lord, and she was going to decide what she was going to do.

Chapter 13

Commitment and determination.
- Rhonda Pierce

N olt typically arrived at the garage between six and seven in the morning. He didn't eat breakfast before he left his house because he just wasn't hungry that early in the morning. Usually around ten is when he started to feel like he needed some food.

At 9:30, his dad came out to the shop where he was working on fixing a broken wheel stud.

"You ready to go?" his dad said, and Nolt looked up.

"I have about ten more minutes here."

His dad nodded and walked off.

Nolt finished up, wondering if his dad had a point with this. It felt odd that they were casually going out for breakfast in the middle of the day. Still, he washed his hands and strode to his dad's office, where his dad was just standing up from his desk.

"You want me to drive?" Nolt offered.

"I will. I have something I need to go look at before we eat anyway."

"Oh. Okay."

He hadn't been expecting that, but it didn't matter. It was probably a part, maybe even a motor or tranny his dad wanted to check out, or even possibly a wreck. Every once in a while, they'd bring one home for parts, which was cheaper than ordering parts or trying to source them at the junkyard.

They met at his dad's truck, and there wasn't much conversation as they pulled out, driving west.

Nolt was curious as to where they were going, because he expected them to go into town and eat at the diner, so this was a bit of a shock.

But he didn't mind. Didn't mind the quietness of the cab, and didn't mind the idea that something might be taking his mind off of what he had done last Saturday night.

Shasta had been beautiful and sweetly modest all evening. Grateful and gracious. He admired her, and she caught him staring several times.

He hadn't meant to.

Just the feeling of the evening and holding her under the stars with the evening air and breeze and feeling her against him, and that kiss...

That's where things had been really good in his head, before they went really bad, because she had taken a chance on him, and he knew he'd hurt her.

He hadn't meant to. And hadn't wanted to, of course.

But he didn't want to go there. Of course, he should have said that, instead of kissing her, and that's where he felt guilty and sort of rotten in the stomach.

Because after she said what she did, he should have said "that's very sweet of you" and given her some kind words before he gently let her down, letting her know that if he was ever in the market for someone he wanted to be more than friends with, she would be at the very top of his list, but he just wasn't.

Instead, he hadn't said anything half so great; he acted like an idiot and a jerk. And that was putting it nicely.

There was also a nagging thought in his head that he would never find anyone half so amazing as Shasta. Not just that, but...he felt pulled toward her like he'd never felt pulled toward another woman before, including Alana. Which made sense since he was older now. He'd know more what he wanted. Someone who wasn't going to cause a lot of drama by getting offended over everything and pouting for days on end. Someone who smiled and laughed and enjoyed herself wherever she was. Someone who admired and respected him, who made him laugh and didn't see him as a project that needed a lot of work.

Someone like Shasta.

But he couldn't be what she needed. Someone young and enthusiastic and in love with life and fun.

It was another fifteen minutes before his dad started to slow down to make a turn to the south.

He didn't say anything, and Nolt didn't ask, but he wasn't familiar with this area and had no idea where they were going.

It wasn't too long before they came to a small town, with a few houses on both sides, and his dad checked a piece of paper he was holding in his pocket before passing a church and pulling into the first house on the other side.

"The fellow here has a furnace for sale, and I thought I'd take a look at it," his dad said casually.

"A furnace?" Nolt said, wondering what in the world his dad needed a furnace for.

"You heard me," his dad said, shifting the truck into park and killing the motor.

Nolt shrugged mentally, unhooked his seatbelt, and got out.

Whatever his dad was up to, he obviously didn't want to talk about it.

Nolt figured he got that way too. Maybe in his head, or just when he didn't want to be questioned about his decisions. Because, man, he couldn't even imagine what in the world his dad needed a furnace for. Was he building a house? A new garage? Maybe he was going to donate it to someone.

They knocked on the door and stood waiting. The television was easy to hear, and Nolt thought he saw two little towheaded boys sitting in front of it through the curtains. He felt a little like he was a peeping Tom, but he was standing on the porch with nothing to do, and that's just where his eyes went.

His dad rapped for a third time before the door opened.

A woman, looking a good bit like she might have just gotten out of bed, with her hair sticking up in different places, wearing an oversized, stained T-shirt over tight yoga pants with a hole in one knee, opened the door.

Nolt stood patiently, waiting for his dad to speak, but then something triggered in his brain, and his eyes jerked back to the woman's face.

"I'm here about the furnace?"

"Uh...that's my boyfriend's. Hang on," she said, then looked over her shoulder and screamed, "Bobby! Get your butt out of bed. The man's here. He came on time, like I told you he would."

She turned back to them. "You guys can stand there on the porch. I told Bobby you would be here when you said you would, but he said everybody's always late. That was just his excuse for not wanting to get up."

As she was talking, her eyes ran up and down Nolt's dad's body, then she turned her gaze on him.

She did the same thing with her eyes, then her brows crinkled a little as they landed back on his face.

The uncomfortable curl that had been building in his stomach tightened like a fist as their eyes met, then his tracked to the berry-shaped birthmark, faint but noticeable, that rested on the side of her face, right by her hairline.

It was unique. It was exactly the birthmark Alana had.

"Nolt?" she said, her voice not any lower than it had been, but her eyes had narrowed.

He swallowed, and he could almost see his dad staring at him, not grinning, because his dad wouldn't want to lord anything over him, but maybe watching curiously.

"Yeah."

"Lana, baby, tell that dude to go around back of the house and check out the furnace, let me know if he's interested. I'm not getting out of bed just to have them come here and kick some tires."

Alana jerked her head. "You heard him."

But instead of going back in and closing the door, she opened the screen door and stepped out. "Although, I'd like to talk to Nolt for a minute." It might have been a question, but it sounded more like a flirtatious suggestion.

"I can show myself to the back of the house," his dad said, walking off the porch and down the steps, and then disappearing in the unkempt yard behind the house.

Nolt noticed Alana's arm, where the name Brandon was tattooed on her arm with a line through it, and the name Bobby tattooed above it.

At least the heart that went around both of them had been big enough to accommodate the change in names.

"It's been a long time," she said, still a lot of flirt in her voice, as she stepped closer.

Thoughts of last night went through Nolt's head, when the woman who had been close to him had been one he wanted. In fact, he remembered thinking he couldn't get close enough. She hadn't even been as close as Alana without him wanting to put his arms around her and draw her nearer, breathe her air and her scent and feel her body against his.

He took a step back. "More than a decade."

"You always were a quiet one," she said, her eyes wiggling up and down. "I'm looking to get away from that loser upstairs, I don't suppose you're looking for a roommate?"

If he hadn't felt so uncomfortable, he might have laughed.

His dad had actually suggested that having one would be beneficial, just last night. Suggested a wife, he corrected himself. Not a roommate.

When he'd seen the way Shasta looked at the horses, he thought maybe that wasn't such a bad idea.

But Alana had been a roadblock in his head.

To have her standing here on her porch propositioning him in the morning... Last night, he would have been excited. Eager.

Reality was a little different.

"No. I'm not."

"I don't see any ring on your finger."

He lifted it and looked at it, like he needed to confirm her words, but he just didn't know what to say.

He hooked his left hand around his neck, rubbing it a bit, and then just decided he didn't really have anything to say.

"Guess I'll go give my dad a hand."

Her face fell, and she wiggled her nose, like she was pouting.

"Fine. If you decide that you're lonely, I'm good company. I also make a great margarita." She winked at him, and he jerked his head as he turned, stepping off the porch and walking around without looking at her again.

He met his dad coming back through the overgrown path from the back of the house.

His dad didn't climb the stairs to the porch but called out, "You can tell your boyfriend that we'll take it. My truck's sitting right there. It said in the ad that he'd load it. My boy and I are going to go up to the restaurant back along Main Street and have some breakfast. If you need a hand getting it on the truck when I get back, I'll help. If he's not around, I'm leaving without it."

"Bobby, did you hear that?" Alana yelled over her shoulder before she turned back around, her eyes landing on Nolt. "Remember what I said."

Nolt jerked his head one last time, then turned with his dad and walked up the street.

They didn't say much as they walked into the diner together.

A waitress, blonde hair up in a ponytail, with pink cheeks and bright red lipstick, took their drink orders and gave them menus.

Nolt waited until she came back and took their food order before he said, "You knew who lived there."

His dad nodded, not even looking sheepish.

"And you brought me on purpose."

His dad nodded again, taking a big drink of his water before he set it down. "I owed you that."

"You owed me?" Nolt felt confused. What did his dad mean by that?

His dad leaned back in the booth seat, his eyes looking at the table but not seeing.

Finally he said, "Your mom ran off when you were young. You don't really remember her, but I made a bad choice." His dad shrugged his shoulders. "Plain and simple—I was dumb."

"It's not your fault."

His mom didn't want to stay. That wasn't his dad's fault. Sure, his dad wasn't perfect. Nolt knew he wasn't perfect. But no one was perfect. His mom chose to leave, instead of staying and keeping the vows she made.

"At this point in time, it doesn't matter about faults. Not any-more. It probably didn't matter at the time. The only thing that really mattered was that she ran off with another man. That meant I had biblical grounds to divorce her. Although I didn't. She's the one who served me papers. Still, I felt like I could look around, find someone."

Nolt nodded, barely remembering. There had been seven young children, his dad ran the trucking company and their feed mill business. There hadn't been much help, and money had been tight.

He didn't realize that bit about the money until he was older, but he did miss his mom.

But his dad wasn't talking about his mom. He was talking about his stepmother.

"When Hazel came into town, she was part of the rodeo that was there over the Fourth of July. She caught my eye, but I never thought anything would happen. After all, I have seven kids."

"I vaguely remember Miss Charlene and Miss Kathy watching us kids so you could go on a date," Nolt said, still not sure how any of this tied in with Alana.

"Yeah. I fell hard that night. But she was on contract with the rodeo and was leaving."

Nolt nodded again and leaned back as the waitress brought their food and asked if they needed anything else.

After she left, his dad picked up his fork. "We talked every night that summer. I was busy, she was busy, but we made time. Because it was important to us both."

"You guys got married at the beginning of November."

"We did. We couldn't wait any longer, even though she wasn't quite finished for the year."

"I guess I never really thought about it, but you really loved her." Nolt felt like an idiot for just realizing that. His memories were all of his mom. How she left them, how devastated he had been. How hard it was to get over the fact that his mom didn't want him.

"I did. And we had a whole year together. I guess that whole year was like a honeymoon with seven kids."

"Looking back at it as an adult, that was a pretty big step for her, to marry a man with seven kids."

"And to love them like they were hers. Because that was the really amazing thing. She stepped into my family and treated my children like they were the most precious things on earth. If I hadn't already been completely enraptured with her, that would have done it."

Nolt didn't have children of his own, so maybe he didn't quite understand, but he supposed he could see what his dad was talking about. "I liked her. I just don't have a whole lot of memories of her."

"You wouldn't. She was busy with the little kids. Plus, she gave trick riding lessons on the side."

Nolt nodded. He didn't know how much his dad was going to say, and he didn't want to trigger any hard memories.

"I don't know if you know this or not, but she was fifteen years younger than I was."

Nolt sat up straight, his eyes widening and his fork frozen in the air. "I didn't realize."

"Yeah. I don't talk about her much." His dad looked at his food. It was unusual for him to have food on his plate and not be eating it, but he just sat there.

Nolt waited.

"The age difference concerned me. She was young. She wanted to see the world. She was energetic and fun, and I was an old man, at least I felt like it around her sometimes, with a family and businesses that tied me to Sweet Water just as tightly as if I had chained myself to the gas pumps at the C-Store." His dad used his fork to push a French fry around on his plate.

"But she took you anyway."

"She did. She decided she was ready to settle down. That's what she said anyway, although I had trouble believing it. And she said she loved kids and wanted more."

That surprised Nolt. He hadn't known it. Had never thought to ask. His dad was just his dad. He didn't think of him as a person with a story, with pain in his past, heartbreak. Love. Because it was obvious his dad had loved Hazel.

"I didn't think my life could get any better. We did hurt for money for a while. Both of my businesses were new, I had a lot of debt, and we had some lean years. I was right on the tail end of those lean years when I married Hazel. We couldn't afford a wedding, nothing grand. We just got married and invited people to bring a dish and celebrate with us."

"Sounds simple."

"It was. And Hazel was happy, although at the time, I said in my head that if I ever had money, we would have another wedding, one where she got the big dress and the pretty flowers and the beautiful church and all the guests and great food and dancing at a reception. I didn't tell her, but I promised myself that."

Nolt's throat tightened. He knew Hazel never got her wedding.

Chapter 14

Compassion and understanding with love.
- Connie J Randel

"**S**he didn't care about the money, and after watching her take care of my kids, which she insisted were now *our* kids, for almost a year, I believed her when she said she truly wanted more." Nolt's dad swallowed, setting his fork down and giving up any pretense of pretending to eat. "We'd only known for a week that she was expecting a child when she fell off a horse and broke her neck."

Nolt had no idea. He set his own fork down and tried to close his mouth but couldn't. He'd not known. He knew his stepmother—they all called her ZZ—always had fun with horses and did tricks she had started teaching him how to do, but since he'd never been on a horse, it was slow going.

He'd known she died in an accident involving horses, and later, he figured out she'd been teaching one of her students how to do something, her on one horse, her student, who was very advanced, on another. But her student had somehow gotten scared, had choked, and something he did spooked the horse ZZ was riding. She'd been dead before anyone had ever gotten to her.

"I didn't know. Didn't know that I lost a little brother or sister in addition to a stepmother."

His dad nodded, was maybe a little choked up, but it had happened a long time ago, twenty years or so. And he sighed, sad but not broken about it, although anyone would have understood if he had been.

"You loved her. And you'll never be able to love anyone else." That was mushy stuff. Things he didn't usually talk to his dad about. But here he was, at thirty-four, finally finding out that he had lost a brother or sister and that his dad had been madly in love with his new wife twenty years ago.

"Well, son, that's part of what I wanted to talk to you about."

That his dad found someone? Couldn't be.

Nolt waited.

His dad picked up a French fry in his fingers and dipped it in ketchup. "For a long time, I didn't think I'd be able to find anyone who fit me like Hazel did. Sure, there was a big age gap between us, and she was a risk-taker while I was more methodical. She was young and carefree, I came with seven kids. She'd never been married, I'd had my wife walk out on me. I really wasn't a good bet, but somehow she saw through all of that and saw something she could fall in love with."

"Dad, you're a good man."

"I'm different now than I was then. I guess that's what I'm saying. It is easy to say that if Hazel had lived, I'd still be married to her. But we don't know how time changes things. You never do. I think sometimes we get stuck on something, maybe it's a human nature thing, or maybe it's just a personality thing, and you've done what I do—we don't want to change. We like where we are, and we have in our heads the way it should have been, and that's how we're going to keep it. Even though life has gone on."

"I think I see."

"And that's a good thing, if you're married. You don't want to be looking around, wondering what you're missing out on, looking for someone else who's better than what you have, always wanting something more, or not being happy with what you've done. In life, you can always find someone who looks better than what you have, always. Maybe they don't have the same faults as the one you're with has, but they have different ones. I promise you they do."

"I believe you."

"Anyway, I realized about five years ago that it was silly to get stuck in the past, to never marry again because I'd been with the perfect woman and no one could compare. Because time makes you look back through rose-colored glasses, but Hazel had her faults the same as I did."

"I remember she hated cleaning the house. It was always dirty. I never heard you guys fight, but I know a few times after you left, she was angry because she hated being cooped up inside doing anything."

Far from making his dad sad, he chuckled. "Yeah. She hated paperwork, hated cleaning, doing anything that kept her from her horses or from you kids. She always had time for you."

"I remember that. She was a lot of fun. I guess I resented the fact that I didn't have a mom, and I never really accepted her the way I probably should have."

"That's understandable. Those things take time. Sometimes you never accept someone else. You always wish your parents were back together, because that's the way humans are programmed. One mom, one dad, forever."

"Who even does that anymore," Nolt said, mostly joking, but it was true. "A one mom, one dad family for a lifetime is pretty rare."

"Anyway, that's what I've been thinking about. Now, that doesn't mean I'm just going to go settle down with the next woman who's available, because getting the wrong woman will make you just as unhappy as not having any woman. Just in a different way."

Nolt nodded thoughtfully. That was true. The wrong woman could make a man's life miserable, just the same as a wrong man could make a woman's life miserable. But once they said vows, miserable or no, you had them between you, and that was it.

"Is that what you decided with Mrs. Baldwin?" Nolt asked, figuring he knew the answer.

"Actually, no. Mrs. Baldwin... She would be a good woman, but I'm pretty sure she's not interested." His dad put a French fry in his mouth, then grabbed his drink.

Nolt wanted to ask a little more about that, because all he knew about his dad's association with Mrs. Baldwin was they went out one night, and then there was what felt like a big explosion in Sweet Water, since everyone seemed to be talking about how the Piece Makers had made a huge error and how his dad and Mrs. Baldwin were the biggest fail since an asteroid killed the dinosaurs.

Or something along those lines.

"Anyway, son. When you graduated from high school, and things happened with you and Alana, I kinda stood back and watched. You're a grown man. You were a man far before you graduated from high school. You needed to make your own mistakes. As much as I wanted to protect you from them. Then with having your brothers coming up behind, and your sister, I guess... I guess I never revisited it, and it wasn't until I saw what was going on with Shasta that I realized that maybe you and I needed to talk."

"You mean, maybe you needed to show me that what I remembered might not be what reality actually was."

"Yeah. That."

Nolt nodded briefly. He supposed every teenager, even boys who didn't have the reputation for drama that girls did, had the capacity to think that whatever love story they were in the middle of was the most epic love story ever.

Combine that with his personality of steadfast devotion, and he'd turned Alana into an idol rather than just the memory she was.

"I could see right away she was fickle. That you would pledge your whole heart and soul, and she'd walk away as soon as she found someone else that was a little better than you. She was always on the lookout for the next newest best thing."

"I never saw that."

"Sometimes we get too close to things, especially when we're young, and we miss major red flags that age and wisdom help us see." His dad chuckled without much humor. "As we get older, we have a tendency to see all the red flags and none of the good."

Nolt could relate to that. The older he had gotten, the more he saw the negative unless he deliberately focused on the positive. He supposed it was a deliberate mindset and a choice.

"You're saying she would never have stayed with me anyway."

"No. She was nice, I still think she's nice, but she's not loyal. You can be friends with someone like that, casual friends, but you don't want to put a ring on the finger of a girl who's not going to keep it there."

Funny how in the last twenty-four hours, he had gone from seeing Alana as the love of his life to someone he'd narrowly escaped making a huge mistake with.

"I guess I should be thankful she ditched me when she did, instead of pining over it."

"Yeah. Even if she were the world's greatest woman, and you had missed out on something really spectacular, I think fifteen years is long enough to wish for what you don't have."

Nolt wasn't sure he agreed with that. "I thought having the wrong woman was worse than having none."

"That's absolutely true. You're right. But I'm not sure I subscribe to the idea that there is only one soul mate. Maybe someone else will work just as well. What you really want is equal amounts of devotion and determination to stick together, no matter what. And it helps if you have a lot of similar beliefs and if you have things in common. That definitely greases the gears and makes things easier."

Nolt wasn't sure he'd have anything in common with someone who was twelve years younger than he was, but he supposed he wouldn't know until he tried to get to know her a little better.

He hoped he hadn't wasted his chance. She'd wanted more last night, and he hadn't done a very graceful job of telling her no. He supposed changing her mind, and, more importantly, letting her know that he changed his mind probably wasn't going to have her falling back into his arms.

In his experience anyway, with cattle, with dogs, with any kind of animal, once they were hurt, it was twice as hard to win them back.

He couldn't imagine a woman would be less complicated or easier.

"I think I've screwed things up pretty bad," he finally said as they finished eating.

"Sometimes we do that," his dad agreed. Unhelpfully.

"Thanks," Nolt said with not a little bit of sarcasm.

"Listen, son. There's only so much I can do for you. You're going to have to fix some of your own mistakes."

"It'd be nice if I could just fix the easy ones and you could help me with the hard ones."

"Keep dreaming," his dad said, sliding to the end of the booth and grabbing the check.

Nolt pulled his wallet out and left a generous tip on the table. He needed to figure out a way to convince Shasta to take a chance on him again.

They drove home, him thinking about romancing a woman and what all that would entail. The age difference scared him a little, but maybe his dad was right, and it really wouldn't matter.

When they got to the shop, Calhoun and Bellamy and their children were there, along with one of their employees and their children, and Nolt talked to them for a while about the truck show they were heading to together before he made it the whole way into the shop.

Brawley came over, and they talked about the truck that had just come in that morning, and the noise it was making, and the things they should check for to see what it could be.

"I put a box of parts up on the loft this morning with the forklift, but we're going to need to rearrange things up there so we can get to them a little better. Where I set it, it wasn't very sturdy," Brawley said after they'd talked about the knocking in the motor for a bit.

"I'll look now before I get into anything else," Nolt said, looking up the stairs, then taking a double take as one of their employee's children, Patsy, a four-year-old, stood on the ledge.

There was no handrailing, and she was heading toward the edge.

Railing was something they had intended to put in, but they just hadn't gotten around to it, since they didn't go up there unless they needed parts.

Normally there was a gate that closed at the bottom of the stairs, but they'd been putting things away from the auction, and someone must have left it unlocked.

Regardless, Nolt didn't waste any time but went running for the steps, taking them two at a time.

Maybe he was too hasty, because as he came barreling up, Patsy looked at him with a deer-in-the-headlights look in her eyes, like she'd done something wrong.

And she probably knew she had, since she'd been there plenty of times before with her dad, who'd worked for them for years, and knew she was not allowed to play up there. Everyone had been very clear about that, because like Brawley had just pointed out, a lot of times there were things up there that were not stacked very firmly.

"It's okay, Patsy. Just stand there, I'll come get you."

Patsy froze, then started to cry and turned around and ran.

Her dad would not be very happy about that, but Nolt blamed himself, since he had scared her, because he had been acting out of his own fear, trying to get to her before she fell off the ledge, and might not have modulated his voice as much as he needed to.

He could hear people calling to her from down below, telling her to stop and turn around, and that's when he realized she'd run behind the shelf where Brawley had set that heavy box of parts, and it tilted dangerously.

The entire shelf tilted back. Nolt thought it was going to be okay, since it was most likely going to right itself, but Patsy had lost her balance and fell into the shelf as she tried to turn around and listen to what the adults were telling her to do.

It shoved the shelf in the other direction, and the box balanced precariously on the top started falling. Patsy was too close to the edge to move in one direction, and she stood directly under the box that was just seconds away from tilting off the shelf.

Nolt didn't think about it too much, but he knew he wasn't going to be able to grab her from the inside of the ledge because there were parts stacked around and he couldn't get to her that way.

So he did the only thing he knew to do. He sprinted the last ten feet to her and shoved her as hard as he could toward the inside of the ledge while he fell backward toward the outside.

Possibly if they'd had a railing, he would have been okay, but as it was, he fell off the edge. And down to the hard concrete below.

Chapter 15

Keeping God as the center of your life, relationship, and
family. Also communication with your spouse is crucial!
- Leah from Ohio

S hasta sat at her table, humming.
　　She put the final touches on the dish that was in front of her
and then held it up to look at the handiwork more closely.

She hadn't been able to decide what decisions to make yesterday;
even when she prayed about it, she just didn't hear God saying
anything in particular. So, she decided to stand still and just wait.

In the meantime, she accepted a few small projects that wouldn't
take long and that wouldn't tie her up if she got a clear direction
on the way she was supposed to go.

The piece had actually been easier than what she thought it
would be, and once again she was grateful to Nolt for the cash
that he'd given her. She'd been eating boxed mac and cheese, with
beans mixed in for protein, and that had kept her food budget
down to the very barest minimum.

The rest of her money she had spent on supplies, hoping that it
would pay off as she got paid for some of the projects she had lined
up for the week.

Her fingers had itched more than once to reply to the email
about the barns. She wanted to say yes and start packing her bags,
but on the other hand, she knew that when she did that, she

probably would never come back to Sweet Water, except maybe to visit.

Funny how she'd only been here a little while and the town felt like home.

Maybe it wasn't so funny after all, when one thought about what the town had done for her. Of course she wanted to stay. She owed these people more than she could ever repay, but at the very least, she could stick around and try.

Her phone buzzed with a text from its place over on the counter where she had left it.

She wanted to be able to focus on her work, and her phone was a distraction.

She almost didn't get it, but she had been expecting an answer about the jobs she said she could do, and feeling pretty good about the piece, she figured it was time to take a break.

It was Sadie, and she smiled at the name, but her smile slid as she read the first words: **Meet me by the bookstore...**

Her eyes widened, and her stomach jumped. She unlocked her phone and pulled up the whole text.

Meet me by the bookstore in five minutes. Bring your purse. We're going to the hospital.

She wiped her fingers on her pants and sent a quick response—**K**—before putting her paints away as carefully as she could, washing her hands, grabbing her purse, and flying out the door. Whatever had happened to Sadie, she would happily drive her to the hospital.

Although, halfway down the stairs, she realized that one of Sadie's brothers could take her. Maybe they'd all left the garage for the day. Maybe she should have brought some kind of towels or bandages or something in case Sadie was bleeding everywhere.

Maybe she had a broken bone. Maybe she should have offered to go to the garage and pick her up.

But as she flew out the door, she saw Sadie's car coming up the street, a lot faster than the twenty-five-miles-per-hour speed limit would allow.

She didn't exactly squeal her tires as she pulled in next to the sidewalk, but she rolled her window down and said, "Get in. Hurry."

Shasta didn't question her but ran around and hopped in the front seat.

"You want me to drive?" she asked as Sadie pulled out before she had her belt on, and she did squeal the tires.

"No."

Shasta looked Sadie over up and down, trying to figure out what the problem was.

"Why are we going to the hospital?" she asked, unable to find anything wrong with her friend.

"Hang on," Sadie replied as she slowed for a pedestrian, then hit the gas as soon as they were past, both hands on the wheel, her eyes glued to the road.

As soon as they hit the edge of town, she accelerated even more and let loose a shaky breath.

"Twenty minutes ago, Nolt fell off the ledge in our garage."

Shasta sucked in a breath. She'd just been in the garage last night, and Sadie didn't have to describe the ledge to her. It was basically the equivalent of falling off a second-story balcony, only onto cement below. Unless he hit something else. There could have been a truck or any type of equipment or parts lying below.

"Is he okay?" It was a stupid question, but what she really meant was, did he die immediately? Although they were racing to the hospital. Was that so that they could all say their last goodbyes?

Her fingers dug into her purse, pinching painfully, but she barely noticed.

"I don't know. He was conscious when the ambulance was there, but his leg was bent in a really weird angle, and his head was bleeding, along with his arm."

"Then there weren't any parts or anything sticking out of his torso?" Shasta didn't know if that was a good question or not. She just wanted all the facts immediately so she could know for sure exactly what was wrong. And how he was going to be, but reason told her that Sadie couldn't tell her.

"He joked before they loaded him up in the ambulance that next time he did it, he was going to use a parachute. So, I think that means... I don't know what that means. I've heard of people being okay, and then swelling in the brain kills them. But I know for sure he has a broken leg." Sadie shivered, and Shasta did too.

His leg was broken for sure, and who knew what they'd find when they got to the hospital.

Chapter 16

God. Prioritizing my time w God to top of all my lists, taking
my issues w my husband to God first before speaking to my
husband, to believe that God is in control, to trust God is in
control of my marriage too - I can submit to my husband
because I trust God. I can love him, be a faithful spouse
because God makes that possible.
- Tamsyn from South Africa

They reached the hospital, and Sadie parked haphazardly in the closest spot she could get.

They were both out of the car and power walking to the hospital mere moments after the motor shut off.

It felt like the automatic door took forever as they slowed long enough to wait for it to open.

Shasta's heart beat hard in her chest, and her hands were clammy. Her stomach folded over on itself, and she had trouble catching her breath.

Nolt was too stubborn to die.

Surely.

But everyone died. No one got out of it.

She hated that thought and pushed it aside. If he did, she'd deal with it. But until he did, she was not going to allow that thought space in her brain.

Dodge and Marigold were already there, along with Nolt's other brothers.

The hospital was small, and the waiting room was empty except for their family.

As Shasta and Sadie walked in, Dodge looked up, recognized them, and started forward.

"Dad's been asking about you," he said, looking at Shasta.

Shasta's eyes widened, and she looked from Dodge to Sadie and back to Dodge.

Dodge was still staring at her.

"Me?" she asked, pointing at her chest like that would help clarify things.

Dodge's mouth twitched, but the stern expression stayed on his face. "Yeah. Sadie can go back with you, but they're only allowing two people in the room at a time. Dad's back there now."

"How is he?" Sadie asked, and if she were upset that Shasta seemed to be getting preferential treatment, she didn't act like it bothered her.

"He's awake. Complaining. He's gonna make it, is what I'd say." Dodge's words were said with an edge of humor, although his face kept its serious expression, maybe because he was the second oldest and felt the responsibility on his shoulders.

Sadie and Shasta digested that while Dodge jerked his head. "Come on. I told the ladies at the desk you guys were on your way."

Shasta wanted to ask how they all beat them there, but maybe they were all at the garage and knew. Or maybe they just drove fast. Whatever, it didn't matter, other than making her feel conspicuous to be the one escorted back to see him when all of his brothers were sitting there in the waiting room.

"These are the two I told you about," Dodge said as they got to the front desk.

The nurse smiled solemnly and pushed a button. The glass doors opened, allowing them access to the long hallway.

"I'll stay out here with the brothers." Dodge spoke as they stopped at the doors. "He's down at the end on the left."

"I don't have to go in, if there's only two people allowed, surely his brothers want to see him."

"No. We've seen him enough. Everyone got to go back and see with our own eyes that he's just as cantankerous as he's always been, just a little bit more bloodied and a little bit crooked right now."

Shasta smiled despite herself, and Sadie shook her head, grinning.

"Your family is so weird," Shasta said under her breath as they walked down the hall.

"I know. It's no wonder I could never get a guy to stay with me for more than three days. Once he met my brothers, it was all over."

"Then don't introduce him to them," Shasta said; it was the same advice she'd given her throughout college.

"I have to. I've told you. If a guy can handle my brothers, then they can handle anything. And that's how I'll know he's worth keeping."

Shasta didn't say anything more. They'd talked about it a lot over the years, since Sadie's brothers were a huge part of her life. And Sadie had said over and over that she didn't want to bring someone into the family that wasn't going to get along. So she wouldn't let herself fall for anyone who wasn't going to fit in.

It didn't sound like her opinion had changed, but it did sound like maybe she was frustrated at how long it seemed to be taking to find someone who liked her *and* her brothers.

They reached the end of the hall and turned left, walking into the end room.

Sadie went first, with Shasta looking over her shoulder. Their dad stood at the foot of the bed, his arms crossed over his chest, his feet braced.

Nolt lay on the bed, looking extremely uncomfortable, although whether that was from pain or from his dad's glare, Shasta couldn't say.

She did notice his face smooth out a little as she walked in.

She tried not to notice, because he'd been very clear the night before about not wanting her.

She hadn't been thinking about that, just worried about him and hoping he was truly okay, wanting to see with her own eyes.

But now that she'd seen him, memories of the kiss came roaring back, along with everything he'd said afterward. All the words about not wanting her, all the rejection, all the disappointment and discouragement and despair.

The nurse on their side of the bed moved a little, her electronic tablet in her hand as she looked at the numbers on the monitors over the top of Nolt's head. "I'd like to see these numbers go down a little. Just lie back and try to relax. Have the pain meds kicked in yet?"

"I'm good," Nolt said, but he didn't look at the nurse. He didn't take his eyes off Shasta.

"I hope they drugged you up good," Sadie said, walking over to the side of the bed opposite the nurse and putting her hand on Nolt's. "I think I can get some good pictures, if they give you enough drugs."

"I think I can run over your phone," Nolt said, and while Shasta heard a bit of the old Nolt in there, his words did sound...not slurred exactly, but lethargic.

Shasta had followed Sadie over to the other side of the bed, and she stood beside her, glancing at Mr. Powers who nodded and smiled.

"I'm glad you could make it. He asked about you."

"I did not," Nolt denied, and the smile that had been forming on Shasta's face died.

Of course he didn't.

"Is your name Shasta?" Mr. Powers asked.

Shasta nodded, wanting, now that she had seen that Nolt was okay, to walk back out of the room, but she didn't want to be rude.

"You're the only Shasta I know, and that's who he was asking for." Mr. Powers gave Nolt a stern look and lifted his brows as though daring him to contradict him again.

Nolt's mouth flattened, but he didn't say anything else.

"Trading places," Sadie said, grabbing a hold of Shasta's shoulders as she slid behind her, pushing her up toward the head of the bed.

The nurse had been writing on her tablet as they'd had their exchange, and she lowered the tablet and looked at Shasta. "Go ahead and touch him. Sometimes that helps lower blood pressure and calms them. He seems agitated, and he was in a lot of pain. I'm not sure if the meds have kicked in or not. He is one of those that it's hard to tell on."

She lifted her brows like she just had to deal with what she got, and when Shasta made no move, she said, "Go on, honey, it's okay. Put your hand over his. Human touch is very calming."

Shasta wanted to say human touch might be calming if you actually want the person to touch you, but she didn't. The nurse probably assumed that she was a sister or a relative because she was back here.

She didn't know what Dodge had said when he told them they were coming.

She didn't want to get thrown out. She wanted to be able to walk out herself, so she took her hand and set it lightly on Nolt's.

She wasn't expecting his hand to twist under hers until it was palm up, and he'd laced their fingers together.

For not wanting her here, it was odd that he had grabbed a hold of her.

The nurse looked at their fingers, smiled, then looked at the numbers above the headboard again. "That's good. That's exactly what we want." She looked at Nolt. "Can I get you anything before I go?"

"I'm good."

The nurse pursed her lips and gave Shasta a look, but Shasta had to hand it to her, she didn't roll her eyes. "The doctor will be in shortly. They're going to want to take you down for x-rays and then go from there depending on what they see."

Nolt nodded, and the nurse gave the three of them a look. "The meds are going to make him sleepy, so don't worry, okay?"

She waited until they all nodded then asked if they had any questions and waited for them to shake their heads before she left.

"Sadie and I are going to walk out for a bit. There's only supposed to be two visitors at a time, and we don't want to take advantage of the nurse's kindness." Mr. Powers spoke to Nolt, but then he looked at Shasta. "Are you okay?"

"I'm fine."

"Hang on a second," Sadie said. "Give me your phone. I'll make up a group text with all of our numbers in it so you can let us all know if anything happens."

Shasta nodded, still feeling a little out of place, like she didn't belong, like she was being given a place of honor that she didn't deserve.

Mr. Powers was acting like she did, and Sadie was being very matter-of-fact about it too. Even Dodge had been expecting her.

She wasn't sure what all that meant, but she didn't want to be rude in the face of their generosity and kindness.

"Here you go. You can mute us if we get too rowdy," Sadie said with a wink.

Mr. Powers raised his brows at that but didn't say anything.

Their footsteps faded away, and Nolt's eyes were closed. Shasta wasn't sure what to do, how long she was going to be staying, and she would like to know the whole story about what happened.

"Sit down." Nolt spoke without opening his eyes.

"They didn't give you enough drugs to take the edge off your bossiness. I hope it's working for your pain anyway," Shasta murmured.

"Just as sassy as she always was," Nolt breathed, his eyes still closed. His words slurred just a bit. "I don't know what they gave me, but it makes my eyelids feel like they weigh a hundred pounds each. Which is too bad, because I want to look at you."

Shasta tried not to let his words affect her. He didn't mean them. Or maybe he just wanted to look at her so he could tell her to leave again.

She needed to get rid of those thoughts. She wasn't going to be bitter and angry just because she wanted him and he didn't want her. She couldn't manipulate people into wanting what she wanted. She couldn't manipulate them into liking her. And she didn't want to. Treating him badly because he'd hurt her was a juvenile thing to do.

Lord, help me be kind. Help me be gracious and treat Nolt the way You want me to. With love and compassion, the way I would treat You if You were here.

It wasn't his fault he didn't feel the same way about her that she felt about him. And it wasn't right for her to be unkind because he'd rejected her.

Taking a breath through her nose, she determined to try with all her heart to forget about the rejection and treat him the way he wanted to be treated, like a friend. One whom she cared for greatly.

"If you'd like me to get you some toothpicks for your eyelids, I can. I combed my hair just for you, you know."

One of his eyelids cracked open, slowly, like it took a lot of effort. "Looks nice."

They fell back closed, like they truly did weigh a lot, but his hand squeezed hers, and she squeezed back.

Another fifteen or twenty minutes passed until they came to take him for his x-rays. The attendant said they might take him directly to the CAT scan afterward but that the doctor would go out to the waiting room when they were done to tell them they could come back and also to let them know what they'd learned. Although the attendant said that they'd have a specialist from a bigger hospital look at the scans before they made any determinations on them.

Shasta nodded and stood, keeping her hands clasped with Nolt's as she looked down on him. Unsure whether he was awake and had heard all that or not. "I'll tell your family what's going on, and I'll be out there with them."

"Do it for me," he mumbled.

"What?" she said, leaning closer.

"Do the x-ray for me."

She laughed a little. "I wish I could."

That was actually true. She'd do it for him if she could. Just because it was most likely going to hurt, a lot. She had been carefully trying not to look at the bulge of the sheet and the way his leg didn't go straight down.

It wasn't off at a right angle, or even a forty-five-degree angle, just not quite right. And it made her stomach hurt to look at it.

The nurse had cleaned up blood that might have been on his face, and while he had a bump around his temple, it didn't look any worse than it might have had he bumped into a cupboard in the kitchen or something.

"Liar," he said, smiling.

"You can think that if you want to," she said.

"I know better. You're a good woman," he mumbled, making Shasta laugh, because he almost sounded drunk.

She exchanged a look with the orderly, who was smiling as well.

"Tell her goodbye for now," the orderly commanded

"You're coming back?"

"Yes. As soon as they let me."

She'd be out in the waiting room as long as she needed to be. And she wouldn't leave. Not if he wanted her to stay.

She was hoping that made her a good friend and not a pathetic woman who was dealing with a serious case of unrequited love.

She walked out first, turning right and going toward the waiting room, but turning around and watching as they turned left out of the room and disappeared around the corner of the hallway.

There was a nurse at the desk right beside the doors, and she smiled at Shasta as she pushed the button for them to open.

"Thanks," Shasta said, watching as Nolt's family stood, waiting for her to walk to them, expectant looks on their faces, wanting her news.

She recognized Coleman Baldwin, who was Nolt's best friend and who had joined the group that included all of Nolt's brothers, along with Marigold.

"They just wheeled him back to get x-rays, and they said they might take him straight to the CAT scan after they were done." She grimaced a little. "He was not looking forward to it, but if the drugs weren't helping with the pain, at least they were making him very sleepy. He didn't really talk at all while I was back there."

"Thanks for going back. He was asking for you, but he might not have remembered," Mr. Powers said, coming forward and putting a hand on her shoulder.

"Of course. He sat with me through my sickness, actually he found me. If it weren't for him, I wouldn't be here right now."

Mr. Powers's look said that he thought there might be a little more to their relationship, but he didn't say anything, dropping his hand from her shoulder.

"Is there a restroom around?" Shasta asked, figuring that if she was going to go back and sit with him, she might as well take care of what she needed to because who knew what the rest of the day would bring.

Sadie pointed it out, and Shasta walked down the hall, thinking that sometimes a person's day just didn't turn out quite the way they thought it would.

Chapter 17

Putting God first! Good communication which means not just telling your side but respecting your spouse enough to truly listen to how they feel. It's too easy to keep the focus on yourself, flip the lens. Perseverance, being committed to staying the course even when things are difficult. Commitment and ease are two different things.
- Anna Bottoms recently moved from Alaska to Ohio

Sadie watched Shasta walk away, then turned to face her brothers and Coleman.

She had a little trouble meeting Coleman's eyes. And she kind of wished he wasn't there, since he always made her self-conscious and uncomfortable.

She didn't know why, since he basically didn't know she existed, which made the crush that she had on him since junior high extremely awkward. But he needed to hear what she had to say anyway.

"I'd like to make sure that Shasta gets to spend as much time with Nolt as possible."

"You want to explain that to us?" Brawley said, lifting a hand up. "I like her. She's nice and everything, but I didn't know there was a thing between the two of them."

"There's not," her dad said. "At least not yet."

"There's never going to be." Coleman's words were confident. "Nolt fell for Alana Lessing, and he's never even looked at anyone else." He lifted his shoulder. "Sorry."

"I wouldn't be so sure about that," her dad said, and Sadie wondered if her dad, of all people, had seen the same thing she'd seen between Nolt and Shasta.

"I agree with that." She took a breath and met Coleman's eyes. "I know you're right. He's loved Alana for years, but with Shasta, I've seen the first glimmer of feeling, and I think he could fall for her, if he'd let himself."

"I think he will," her dad said again.

She asked, "Did you talk to him?"

"Let's just say we had a conversation that opened his eyes. I don't know if anything will come of it, but I do believe Shasta can handle him, and he definitely has some pretty strong feelings for her."

Coleman shoved a hand in his pocket and looked a little bit like he didn't believe it, but he also seemed to be thinking about what they were saying.

"You're saying you want to have Shasta be the spokesperson for the family?" Flynn asked, always studious and quiet and always wanting to make sure he got things accurate.

"Is that okay, Dad?"

"I think it's a good idea. I would say, if we want, we could stay for the results of the CAT scan, but we all know he didn't hit his head that hard. It's that broken leg that could be a problem."

"He's not going to die from a broken leg." Silas stated the obvious.

"That's right. And I think Shasta feels like she owes him, since he took care of her, and I was thinking that having them spend that much time together might encourage them in the direction they're already heading."

"Since when did you become a matchmaker?" Dodge asked, his arm around his wife, holding her close to him, but his expression almost aghast, like he didn't recognize his own father.

"How do you know I haven't been one all along?" Mr. Powers said, lifting his cowboy hat from the chair and settling it on his head. "I'm going to head home. I'd appreciate knowing if there are any changes. You did include me on that group text, right?"

Sadie nodded, appreciating the fact that their dad was concerned, making sure his kid was okay, but didn't feel the need to push in front and take over a spot that might better be filled by someone else.

Chapter 18

Communication - seems harder for the males!
- Teresa Fordice from Indiana

S hasta came down the hall from the restroom, smiling at the receptionist and fighting the odd feeling that she didn't belong in a hospital.

The Powers brothers all moved like they were getting ready to head out. Flynn, the youngest brother, came over and put a hand on Shasta's shoulder.

"Nolt's a great guy, but you might have to develop a tough skin. Sometimes he gets carried away with being bossy and forgets to be considerate and can be a little abrasive." Then his serious eyes narrowed. "If you can handle it, I think you'll be good for him."

"Yeah, Nolt's like an old man. He needs someone a little younger and more exciting. Maybe you can liven him up some," Brawley said, smirking as he went by and clapping Shasta on the arm.

Coleman stopped in front of her, and Shasta was tempted to grip Sadie's hand. Sadie had mentioned more than once in college how she totally crushed on her oldest brother's best friend.

She always said that any man who was interested in her couldn't put up with her family, but Shasta often wondered if it wasn't because she was just trying to find an excuse to dump them, since no one could measure up to Coleman.

"You two went to school together, didn't you?" he asked, looking at Shasta and jerking his head at Sadie.

Shasta wanted to put an arm around her friend, because she was absolutely right, Coleman barely noticed she was alive.

"That's right," Shasta said.

That seemed to be all he wanted to know about that, since his next sentence was a completely different subject. "If it's okay, I'll tell one of the brothers that they'll need to come in and pick up Sadie. They can drive your car in and leave it here."

"That's fine. If you don't mind?" She looked at Sadie for confirmation.

Sadie nodded. "They could even bring Nolt's pickup in, if that might be easier for him to get into right now."

"I don't know if I'm comfortable driving that."

"It might be too high for him to be able to get into anyway," Coleman pointed out. "Although, your car might be low to get out of. I think we'll go with what you're comfortable with. He can sit in the back seat, and if he can't get out, he's got enough brothers that can come give him a hand."

"They'll never let him live it down, but they'll give him a hand," Sadie said, mostly under her breath, which was rather unlike Sadie, but Shasta chalked it up to her being around Coleman and him making her nervous.

Sadie stood beside her while everyone else left, with Mr. Powers being the last.

"I know I'm not wrong about how my son feels. Pretty confident about you as well."

"I don't want to argue, so I'll take your word for it," Shasta said, even though she had trouble believing him. "I can tell you that I'll do my best to take care of him and do whatever he needs."

"I wouldn't be leaving if I didn't believe that."

"Thanks for giving me the opportunity to pay him back for what he did for me."

"I figured that might be in your head too." Mr. Powers grinned.

He left shortly after. The waiting room seemed empty and quiet after all the noise, and Shasta began to doubt herself as to whether she could handle this on her own.

Not that everyone wouldn't come running back if she so much as looked like she wanted them to, but they seemed to think that she would be able to get Nolt to do what the doctor said, to get him to talk to her, to get along with him.

They'd done okay together when it had been her that had been laid up. But something told her it may be a little different now that he was the one who needed help.

"Are you okay?" Sadie asked, glancing at Shasta's lap where her fingers twisted together.

"I think so. It's just kind of crazy how everyone was here, and then they all left."

"I think they all just needed to make sure that he wasn't going to die, and I also think that as tough as guys like to make themselves out to be, they all have a little bit of a romantic spot." Sadie laughed. "Or maybe they are really desperate to get Nolt married off and have him get some kind of softness in his life."

Shasta laughed. But the sound rang hollow because she knew that Nolt had already rejected her. Even though she'd determined that it wasn't going to bother her, the fact remained that any kind of matchmaking, or hopes for romance, was destined to be not realized.

Maybe it just showed how much she wanted to be with him, since she really hadn't put up much of a fight to not stay, even though she knew their efforts were wasted.

"I guess that's one way to look at it," she said, not committing to being the romantic interest.

"I think I'm going to walk around the parking lot for a bit while I wait, get some fresh air. I'll text you when your car is here, in case you need to leave and go somewhere."

"That's good. They didn't say whether they were going to keep him tonight or not..."

"I hadn't heard either, but don't be afraid to call the family if you need to go home or just get fed up with him. Everyone will understand."

"I can't quit. He didn't get fed up with me, and I can be pretty difficult sometimes."

"I think Nolt's name is in the dictionary next to the word difficult." Sadie adjusted her purse strap. "If you're going to be okay, I'll head out now. Hopefully whoever's bringing your car doesn't take too long. I should get back to my desk. I've been spending a lot of time away from it lately."

Sadie reached out to hug her, and Shasta returned it. Holding tight for just a moment.

Wondering what it would be like to have a family like Sadie had. Sure, she didn't have a mom who adored her or a dad who was wise and unselfish. But her dad clearly cared for her, as did her brothers.

Sadie always had been very intuitive, and as she pulled back, she said, "I'm really hoping that things work out between you and Nolt, because I always wanted you to be part of our family. Although, I never matched you up with Nolt in my head. Any of the other brothers, I could see you with. But Nolt? He's tough."

The part of Shasta that loved to rise to a challenge wanted to say, "I've got this," but that was arrogant and exceptionally untrue. She didn't have anything. Except words of rejection, and a desire to ignore them and be kind anyway.

"I'm tough too," she said, making sure she had an easy, happy look on her face.

That was true anyway. Even if she didn't feel tough all the time.

She'd been through a lot, and it was true that every hard thing a person went through made them stronger.

Sadie walked out, and Shasta sat down on one of the hard plastic chairs to wait for the doctor. Thinking about the irony of her finally having work and being unable to do it.

While she was waiting, she could send a few emails and messages letting people know that the things she'd agreed to do might be a little later than she had estimated.

Chapter 19

Honesty, Trust and Loyalty.
- Pam from DE

The pain wouldn't let him sleep.

Nolt still felt heavy, and his limbs were weighted but also floating. An odd sensation. His brain felt like it was stuffed with cotton, but it was his leg that sent searing pain all over his body. He could feel it with every beat of his heart, shooting pain curled around his waist and squeezed his rib cage.

It made his head hurt. He might not be able to open his eyes, and when they were shut, he saw red, like blood, hot and thumping.

It was mostly his fault, since they'd given him something for the pain, but he had asked to not take anything more, and when they asked him how he felt, he told them he was fine.

He hated drugs, hated not being in control of his mind, hated this cottony, lethargic feeling that made him want to act like a two-year-old, rolling around and begging everyone he saw to take the pain away.

So far, he'd been able to keep his mouth shut.

A soft hand moved over his, and without thinking, he turned his over so their fingers could thread together like they'd done earlier. He'd seen the surprise on her face. Figured he knew what it was from, because he'd told her clearly that he wasn't interested in her. It was a rejection that she wouldn't soon forget, if he knew anything at all about women.

Which he really didn't. But if she were a man, he'd just flat-out tell her he hadn't meant it, he was sorry, and after thinking about it, he'd like to take it all back.

A man would be fine with that, and they'd be friends right now.

A woman... He was pretty sure it was going to take more than just some pretty words to convince her that he'd changed his mind. And even more to convince her that he was worth taking a chance on again.

"You're awake?" he said, his voice sounding groggy, but at least the words weren't as hard to push out as they had been earlier.

"I've been awake. You sounded restless. Are you in pain?"

"I don't want to talk about pain."

"Well, let's give the man whatever he wants."

Her voice was a little sarcastic, and if they were keeping score, that would be a point for her.

"I'm the one that's sick in the hospital bed. Aren't I supposed to be the one getting whatever I want?"

"You can have as much pain medicine as you want. We have to be able to talk about it in order to give it to you."

"I don't want any. But I don't mind talking."

Or having her talk. Anything to get his mind off how badly he hurt.

"Go ahead. I'll listen."

"Why wouldn't you tell me that you were a foster kid?"

That bothered him. Even when he didn't want to like her, it had bothered him that she wouldn't trust him with that information. It bothered him even more that she told others about it and still hadn't told him.

And he was irritated that he was bothered because something like that didn't normally bother him.

Go figure.

"I guess I didn't think you wanted to know." Her words sounded a little unsure, and he figured he knew why.

"I asked you twice, not necessarily about being a foster kid, but about your past. You wouldn't talk."

"I guess I felt like I was at a distinct disadvantage. Because, having been friends with Sadie, I knew you had pretty much the perfect life."

"She didn't tell you our mom left when we were just little? Sadie doesn't even have any memories of Mom."

"She told me that. I guess... I guess it just felt like she had so many older siblings that it didn't really matter."

"Surely as a foster kid, you know that a mother's rejection stings, for a long time."

"I know." She sounded sorry, sad, maybe reflective. He couldn't get his eyes to stay open long enough for him to read her expression.

"Do you know your parents?"

"I don't know my dad at all. And my mom left me with my grandparents, but they were older. I was probably ten when they had to go to a nursing home, and I went into the system."

Her voice was dispassionate, flat. And he supposed it was one of those things that she couldn't get emotional about or she'd be overemotional about it.

For him, anyway. He was much better off if he just kept his emotions out of the situation and spoke like he didn't care.

"That's young."

"Actually, it's not. I would have been better off being younger. People want cuddly little babies, or cute toddlers, or even elementary school kids. They don't want someone who's a preteen with an attitude."

"I can't imagine you with an attitude."

"Really?" she asked, insinuating that she had one while he was taking care of her.

She really hadn't. She'd been a little grumpy at times, maybe, but if she felt even half as bad as he did right now, it was a wonder she didn't take a knife and slash his arm.

Not that he wanted to do that to her, he just felt irritable and restless and tired. But in too much pain to sleep.

"I went through a series of temporary foster homes, I think one or two of them might have kept me, but there was always something. You know how it goes? Like it seems like the bad things always happen to the best people. I don't know why."

He thought of his dad, losing his second wife, whom he loved. After his first wife had already walked out on him.

His dad hadn't said it, but it had reminded Nolt that time was short. Life didn't last forever. The time that a person is given to spend with someone they love should be cherished. And not taken for granted.

He thought about his brothers, his sister, his dad. He hadn't even known that his dad was looking at someone else. He'd been too wrapped up in himself. Too wrapped up in Alana and nursing his heartbreak.

"I guess I can agree with you there. Look at me. A good person, the best of my brothers. Why am I the one with the broken leg?"

She laughed, and he relished the sound. Loving that she didn't feel the need to giggle behind her hand or something, but loved to laugh.

"I missed it. How did you get to stay? Don't they kick people out when visiting hours are over?"

"I think you were passed out. Either that or sleeping."

The x-ray had been the most painful experience of his life so far. But he wasn't going to say that to her. He didn't want her to go to the nurse and tell her that he needed more drugs.

"So you bribed someone?"

"No, the hospital physician is a friend of Coleman's. I think, maybe even if you didn't have that connection, he might have let me stay anyway. No one came around to kick me out, but I had permission and a name to give if they did."

"You don't have a ride to get home."

"One of your brothers brought my car to the hospital and drove back with Sadie."

"They should have taken my pickup."

"I think Sadie suggested that, but I said I wasn't comfortable driving it, and I would prefer my car."

"So from foster care, how did you end up here?"

It was a sharp change of subject, but...he was curious. And not really capable of focus right now, anyway.

"I don't know if you know this about the foster care system, but when you turn eighteen, you age out. I could go to college for free. So I did. It was just one of God's gifts to me that I ended up roommates with Sadie. We hit it off and spent four years rooming together."

"You sound happy when you're talking about college."

"It was probably the happiest time of my life. I had freedom, but not too much, I didn't have to worry about money, because I had a part-time job that paid for everything I needed, and my education was free. I suppose if I had to do it again, I would have chosen a major with better job prospects than what I did, but I can't deny I had fun."

He felt a bit of jealousy, and he tried to pinch it off. "Lots of boys in college."

"There are."

The machines behind him whirled as his blood pressure cuff filled up, squeezing his arm.

"You dated a lot?"

He shouldn't have asked that. He didn't have any business asking that. Although, he supposed he didn't have any business asking anything. But at least when he was thinking about her, his leg wasn't bothering him so bad.

"Some."

"But?"

"Well, if you must know, Sadie was stuck on someone, and no one that she dated measured up to him. And I didn't like to go places without Sadie, and...hearing her talk about her family, her brothers, and how wonderful you all were made the boys at college seem like just that...boys."

"Interesting."

"Yeah. I don't want you to get a big head, so I wasn't going to say anything, but it's true. I suppose, kids are taking longer to grow up than they used to. Maybe because I was a foster kid, or I don't know. Maybe I just have an old personality, but I felt like college just enables that for the most part. Maybe some girls are happy with boys that don't really have an interest in doing anything other than playing and having a good time, but that just didn't interest me."

"You don't like to play and have a good time?"

"Of course I do. I know you probably didn't see that because I was sick most of the time I was around you, but laughing is fun. I'd much rather be happy than angry, but... I don't want some dude that doesn't know how to be serious once in a while, you know?"

He probably had the opposite problem. It was hard for him to cut loose and have a good time. His mind was always on the work that needed to be done and the responsibilities that had fallen on his shoulders from a young age. It wasn't that his dad wasn't involved in the business, it was that his dad had made sure all of them were involved in the business too, giving them responsibilities that most people wouldn't allow children to have.

He felt it had been good for him. And that, along with his naturally serious, commanding personality, hadn't left much room for goofing off.

"I hadn't noticed. But now that you mention it, I guess when Sadie talked about you, she never talked about parties or either of you doing crazy things."

"Yeah. I figured you hadn't noticed."

Chapter 20

Kind communication.
- Yvette Koke-Curtis from St. Augustine, FL

S hasta hated that her voice sounded sad. She didn't want to dwell on the past. Of course it had been harder, and maybe that's part of what had drawn Sadie and her together. Sadie was pining over Coleman, and Shasta always seemed to be drawn to Nolt. Whatever story Sadie told about her brothers, Shasta always listened for Nolt's name.

But like Coleman and Sadie, Nolt hadn't even known she existed. Quite literally.

She didn't want to keep talking about her past. She hadn't wanted to start, but the way Nolt was tensed, the way he gripped her hand, the way he'd been restlessly dozing, made her think that the pain was worse than he was letting on, and he was talking to her to try to get his mind off of it.

She wanted to help however she could. If that meant she talked about things she didn't want to, then she'd do it, just to try to help.

"There was one foster family I was with not even for a year, just a place to stay until they could find someone who would be more permanent. And they had horses. That was pretty exciting for me, because I'd never been around horses before. Even though it was Nebraska, I was mostly in towns and even spent some time in Lincoln at a foster home there."

"Did you get your own horse?"

"No. They mostly boarded them, but the other thing that was really great about that house was the mom was an artist. It was the husband who took care of the horses, and the wife painted them."

"And you're naturally talented. I've seen your work."

"Horses are my thing. They're harder to paint than what you think. They... There is a spirit about them that's hard to capture. But flowers, I can do that."

"I think you could do horses. Have you tried again since you were there?"

"Sure. I did all kinds of things for my degree, not just painting. I guess I got better. But I just know that's where my love started. At that foster place, so I guess being shuffled around from place to place was good in some ways."

"God knew what he was doing?"

"Sometimes I wonder." He probably couldn't see her sad smile in the dark. She often wondered why she didn't have a foundation, a stable start. Someplace to put her roots. She felt...not grounded.

"Why didn't you ever come home with Sadie? For holidays and stuff?"

"I did once." Sadie had taken all of her roommates home that year for Thanksgiving. "But usually they had trouble keeping people on campus to do the jobs that need to be done on a regular basis. I always volunteered for those, since I didn't have a family to miss."

"That's sad. And I guess I do remember Sadie bringing a bunch of girls home, but I tried to avoid them as much as I could."

"Yeah." She'd noticed. Nolt had come to eat, and he helped clean up, but he disappeared after that. Much to her disappointment. Back then, she thought she might be able to get up enough nerve to strike up a conversation with him, but he hadn't been around long enough for her to test the theory.

"Did you have any other foster homes that helped you with your creativity?"

"No. Not really. That was the only one where anyone was even a little artsy. Although my favorite place, one of the places that might have kept me if they could, the wife there cooked." She never knew whether to call them the wife or mom or stick a Mr. and Mrs. in front of their name. They had preferences, but they never felt like her parents. Although, she supposed that house felt more like an actual family with actual parents than anyone.

"Why didn't they keep you?"

"She got sick and had to go to the hospital."

"That's unfortunate."

"Yeah. Even then, I think she wanted to keep me, but the state wouldn't let her. I was still only fourteen or so. I wanted to take care of her, but they insisted that I needed to be a child in the home, not a caretaker. Or something like that."

"So you learned to paint at one house, and you learned to cook at a different one?"

Shasta smiled, remembering the woman's gnarled hands on a rolling pin as she rolled out the dough for bierocks. She could still hear her voice talking about how her grandmother had taught her how to make them, and now she was teaching Shasta. Those were one of the few precious memories she had of her growing-up years.

"Yeah. I learned to cook."

"Sounds like you like to cook almost as much as you like to paint."

"I wasn't there for very long, but yeah. She made really delicious bierocks. I still remember her rolling them out, telling me about her family, her grandmother and her mother, and I started to feel like I had roots. I learned to make the dish that meant so much to her. It's everywhere in Nebraska. People love it."

"I've never heard of it."

"It's actually very simple. Just cabbage and beef and onions and some seasonings wrapped in an outer crust. Kind of like a stromboli, only with German ingredients."

"Sounds interesting."

"And good. Super delicious. She said her German ancestors made it because it was frugal and filling and delicious." She could still hear her saying those words.

"I can hear your voice change when you talk about her."

"Yeah. I loved her. I wish I would have kept her information. I don't even know if she's still alive. But maybe that was just a feeling of home and family too. You know? I've always wanted that."

Maybe that's part of the reason she was serious in college and drawn to other people who were serious because she was serious.

She didn't want to play and waste her opportunity for education. Or do things that she might regret for the rest of her life. She always had the mindset that she was building a life. She hadn't gotten to the point where she wanted to ruin it.

"I didn't give you credit for who you are. I judged you based on your age."

"I know."

"I'm sorry."

"It's okay. I think stereotypes are stereotypes for a reason. You would have been right about ninety-five percent of the population. So, I guess maybe when you don't fit into a stereotype, it's almost a given that people are going to make assumptions about you that aren't true."

"That doesn't bother you? It's discrimination or whatever."

"I don't think anyone enjoys being misunderstood, but that's something that's gonna happen from now until the end of time. You're going to be misunderstood. People are going to assume things about you that aren't true. People are going to be wrong. People are going to not give you what you want. Life isn't going to be fair. It's going to be hard. You're going to get hurt. Those are all givens."

She wished they weren't. She wished it wasn't true. But then what would the point of life be, if there was no struggle? How would she grow, if she never had the opportunity? Without the pain, she wouldn't appreciate having no pain. Without the struggle, she wouldn't appreciate the victory. Without unkindness and discrimination, she wouldn't be able to appreciate people who were truly kind.

"You're telling me it wasn't stupidity that had me falling off the top of the ledge, it was just a given that there's going to be pain in life?"

"I'm so glad you understood what I was saying."

"What can I say? You're a good teacher."

"Hardly." That was one thing she'd never been good at. "I had a little sister at one of the foster homes, and I had to teach her how to tie her shoes. She never did learn, not the whole time I was there, and every time I tried to teach her, I ended up crying."

"Ouch. A classroom of third graders would rip you to shreds."

"I know. Someone told me I should go for art education, and I knew that was not happening."

"It's probably hard to find jobs in that area as well."

"What good would the job do if I wasn't any good at it?"

"You don't want kids?"

"I do. But it's going to be up to my husband to do all the teaching."

He actually laughed, then coughed, then groaned. "Do not do that again."

"Hurt?"

"Yeah."

She put her other hand on top of their clasped ones and rubbed it over his skin which wasn't rough but was so different than hers. "Let them give you something for it."

"I hate drugs. Hate the way I feel. Hate the way I act on them."

"I'll be here. I'll take care of you. You'll be able to sleep better if you just let them give you something."

He was quiet for a bit, and she thought maybe he was thinking about what she said.

He took a slow breath. "You teach me how to cook your bierocks, and I'll page the nurse and ask for pain meds."

She didn't need a second invitation and agreed immediately.

They paged the nurse, and within ten minutes, she had come and given him something to relax him and help him to sleep.

"You're going to be here in the morning, and you're not going to laugh at me when I act like an idiot because of the drugs," he said, after the nurse left, his voice already sounding groggier.

"Wait. I never agreed not to laugh at you. I also never agreed not to videotape it and send it to the group chat," she said.

"You double-crossed me," he ground out.

"No. I just said I would be here. And I will teach you how to make bierocks. That was the deal."

"You're fired."

"Sorry. I don't know what's up with your family, but they all seem to think that they left you in good hands when they left you with me."

"They did." One of his eyes cracked open, although it was too dark for her to meet his gaze.

"So relax. You'll only be embarrassed for a little while."

He snorted. "Those bierocks had better be worth it."

"I have a feeling you'll eat anything. And these are exceptionally good, so you will love them."

"That's probably not all I'm going to love," he said, his eyes closed, his voice slurring.

She didn't say anything, but the stroking that she'd been doing on his hands stopped while she held her breath.

"I know why my family wanted you here."

"Yeah, me too. They wanted you to have the best nurse there was, and...well, that couldn't be it."

He snorted again. "You couldn't do nursing any better than teaching, right?"

"Unfortunately. I fainted twice in biology class in high school. They finally pulled me out and let me just do bookwork, because I was a liability to the school since the last time I fell, I cracked my head open and bled for an hour. They took me to the ER, and I got fifteen stitches on my head. Sometime I'll show you the scar."

"Not tonight."

"No. Not tonight," she agreed and smiled as his breathing became regular.

He insisted on knowing so much about her, and she supposed she knew him because of Sadie, but someday when he was feeling better, she hoped he would talk to her about himself. Because she was curious too.

Chapter 21

Communication.
- Keisha Taylor from Kentucky

"**I**'m doing fine on my own. You don't have to stay here any-more."

Nolt was sitting up in bed when Shasta walked in a week after he'd been discharged from the hospital.

He'd only been in one night; they put the cast on the next day and wanted to send him to rehab, but when she told the doctor that she was staying with him at his home, and Nolt had agreed to physical therapy four times a week, he'd been allowed to go home, with strict instructions he needed to follow the doctor's orders to the letter so his femur healed properly.

"I promised the doctor that I would stay until the cast was off. I'm not breaking that promise."

"Sadie just accidentally sent me a text that was meant for you." He sat there with his brows raised, his head lowered, glowering at her from his bed, like she was supposed to be scared of him or something.

Normally, she got him out of bed, and he could make it to the bathroom mostly on his own, using a walker. At first, it had been less jarring on his leg for him to use a walker on one side, leaning on her on the other, but the pain had diminished, and she became unnecessary.

When she got him to the bathroom, he'd been able to take care of everything himself, and there hadn't been any scenes like the one she'd experienced with him at her apartment.

She felt the heat crawling up her neck at the thought.

"Well, Sadie needs to be more careful with her phone then," she said, moving the walker over beside the bed.

Thankfully, he owned a ranch house that didn't have stairs, or he'd have been sleeping on the couch for the last week.

The second bedroom in the house was where she'd made herself at home, although for the first few nights, she wouldn't tell him but she'd slept curled in a ball in the hall with his door cracked. She hadn't wanted to miss anything.

"Don't you want to know what the text said?" he said, and she had the feeling he was angry and trying not to show it.

"If it will make you happy, go ahead and tell me what the text said, and then we can get on with our day."

"Stop talking to me like you're the teacher and I'm your student."

"I'm a terrible teacher, remember?"

"You know what I mean."

Her lips worked up, and she thought she saw the corner of one of his tremble.

When she didn't say anything, he lifted his phone, making no move to get out of bed.

She craned her neck to read the text.

I'm sorry you had to tell the barn murals no. You'd wanted to do that forever. And it was such an opportunity. Was there a chance he'd wait?

"Are you going to tell me what this is about?" he asked, and he didn't do quite as good of a job of keeping the anger out of his voice that time.

"The man who bought one of the horses at the auction wanted me to paint some of his barns. Apparently he goes around buying them and fixing them up, and he liked my painting, and he wanted me to do some of them." She shrugged her shoulders. "It's no big deal."

"It's a big deal. Don't you remember when I met you, you were lying on the floor almost dead because you didn't have enough money to go to the doctor? I'm guessing that painting barn murals, especially for a man who is basically collecting barns because he doesn't know what else to do with his money, would be a very lucrative occupation. You can't turn it down."

"I already did." She put her hands on her hips. "Now. Are you going to get out of bed? Or can I go back to the kitchen and finish thawing out the hamburger?"

"Answer my question first, then I'll get out."

"No."

"Is there a reason other than me?" he asked, his eyes narrowed, and for the first time, she realized his anger was more directed at himself. Because he was the reason she'd lost the work.

"Of course. I love Sweet Water. I want to be able to stay here. And when this happened," she nodded her head at his leg, "I'd been praying about whether or not I should accept that. I didn't want to leave, but it was the best opportunity I had to earn money. Then, you fell off the ledge..."

She gave him a look, gently trying to tease him out of his irritation. "Or maybe God knocked you off." She got a smile, which was exactly what she wanted, and she kept going. "And he gave me my answer. When your family asked me to stay with you and be your personal care aide, for as long as you needed it, I knew I couldn't do both, and while this job pays less," a good bit less, "than that one, it enabled me to stay in Sweet Water. Which is where I wanted to be."

"How do you know this wasn't a test? Maybe God just wanted to see if you would be tempted to stay."

"I think it's probably the other way around. The money for the barns was tempting, but I know this is where I'm meant to be.

Sweet Water feels like home. I haven't even been here that long. And I like almost all the people here too."

"Almost all? Really? We have to go there? And here, you gave me this big long lecture about how you are more mature than most people your age and how I should remember that and how I didn't notice it, and so therefore there was something wrong with me—"

"Wait. You are totally making all that up. We never had a conversation like that."

"We did so."

"You are in rare form today. I think maybe somebody needs to break your other leg, because you're a lot quieter when you're in pain."

"Go ahead and try." He grinned, and it was the kind of grin that made her stomach flip and shimmy a little. "You might end up in my lap."

"All right. I'll have to be satisfied with grabbing a cast-iron skillet and smacking you over the head with it."

"It's a good thing I don't have any cast-iron skillets."

"You don't what?"

"I can't believe you haven't noticed that."

"Someone hasn't had a very big appetite, and the entire town of Sweet Water has done to you what they did to me, which was pretty much cook all the food in their pantry and drop it off at your doorstep."

"But we're still cooking today?"

"Yeah, I gave some food to Peyton, and she said she had some older ladies who came in who might be able to use it. Plus, her son was going to have friends over, and you know how preteen boys eat."

"I do. I recall being one of those at one point."

He had to be careful getting out of bed, and she watched, although she didn't reach out to help him. It wasn't that it irritated him so much, she just didn't want him to think that she thought he was some kind of invalid or a baby who couldn't do anything for himself.

He'd actually taken to the broken leg a lot better than she thought he would. The lack of mobility had been frustrating, but it hadn't made him grumpy. Although, yesterday she'd noticed he seemed to be getting bored, and while they played games every day and even read aloud to each other, he wanted to move more. That's why she'd suggested she make a trip to the grocery store yesterday evening and pick up the ingredients they needed to make the bierocks.

Once he was up and had made it to the bathroom, she busied herself with making the bed and straightening the pillows and night table.

He only had his Bible and a small notebook and his bottle of Tylenol.

Still, she needed something to do to stay busy, because she worried that he might fall.

Not that she wasn't sure that between the two of them they could get him back up, she just knew it would be an excruciatingly painful experience for him, and she didn't want it to happen.

The first few days he'd been home, he'd mostly slept, and it had only been in the last few that he'd been up and around.

She'd pretty much successfully put his rejection aside and treated him the way she would any friend. As kind as she could be, a little funny and sarcastic when the opportunity presented itself, and once in a while, something a little flirty came out. She didn't mean for it to, and he never acted like he noticed. Although he never flirted back.

But Nolt wasn't exactly the kind of man who flirted.

He wasn't the kind of man who was meant to be stuck in the house either, and she knew in another week or two, it was going to be a hard job to keep him contained.

Chapter 22

Work. Couples must decide to work together to make a marriage work. It's like being in a rowboat. If you are rowing together in unison the boat will go where you direct it. If the couple are rowing in two different directions the boat does not go forward.
- Sheila Bryant from SC

"I know how to cook hamburger." Nolt allowed himself to look offended. Actually, he hardly ever cooked hamburger. He could do burgers on the grill, along with hot dogs, pretty well. But he didn't do much cooking for himself.

He made sandwiches and supplemented that with odds and ends and a few meals every week at Patty's Diner.

How hard could it be?

"Have you ever cooked hamburger before?"

"Of course," he said, like she'd asked him a ridiculous question. Hopefully she didn't ask for specifics.

"Not hamburgers as in patties. Loose hamburger."

"I'm pretty sure I have."

"So you haven't?"

"I don't know." He took the package, broke the plastic seal, and dumped it into the skillet.

"So... Did you want some pointers on that, or are you just going to go ahead and cook it your way?"

"Don't worry. I'll get it done," he said, trying to keep himself from smiling. Turn the burner on, make it get hot, and eventually the hamburger would cook, right? "What do you want me to do while that's heating up?"

She laughed a little, shaking her head, and then offered him a knife and an onion. "How do you feel about cutting this up?"

"I feel good," he said, using the walker to help him move from the stove to the island counter behind him, taking the onion from her hand, and grabbing the cutting board.

"You know, when we were in the hospital, I told you all about my background and answered all of your questions. I think you should tell me about you today."

Normally, Shasta looked happy, and her voice reflected the joy she had in life.

Just now, her voice sounded a little insecure, like she was afraid he was going to tell her no.

He didn't like that. That she didn't know whether she could count on him or not. That she didn't know all she had to do was ask and he would do whatever he could for her.

"You know my mother ran off when Sadie was a baby." He cut the ends off the onion and chopped it in two, peeling it. He hadn't done too many onions, but he was pretty confident in this at least. "I don't know where she is. None of us do. She didn't stay in touch. It's like one day she woke up and decided she didn't want to be a mom anymore, caught the closest man, and ran off with him. I don't even know if she met him before that day. I think Dad knows who she ran off with, but if he kept tabs on her, I don't know about it."

"That must have been so hard for your dad."

"It was. Partly because she was homeschooling us, but also because he was trying to run two businesses, and money was tight. He couldn't really hire anyone, and yeah. He sent us all to school for a while, but he needed us to help in the business, so he brought us home. The ladies in Sweet Water helped out though, and in all, I think it was probably a good experience. Just...painful."

He got the same tone in his voice that she had had in hers when she was talking about her past. He didn't put a lot of drama in it, just stated it matter-of-factly. It was pretty obvious that it hurt; there was no point in stating it. Nothing anyone could do about it anyway.

"Is this good enough?" he asked, already having half the onion sliced.

"Looks perfect. Um, do you mind if I stir the meat? Or do you prefer it blackened?" she said, scratching her head like she was truly waiting on his answer.

"You're so funny."

"I like to think so." She gave him a grin and wink as she walked by him to the stove and stirred the meat which hissed and gave him the idea that maybe he'd waited slightly too long, but he didn't know the meat needed to be stirred. When he made hamburgers, he just cooked them on both sides.

She grabbed the cabbage that she'd been cutting and put it in the skillet.

"Am I getting behind?"

"You're fine. We'll wait on you."

"We? Like you and the hamburger will wait on me?"

"You were talking about your mom. Want to keep doing that?"

He grinned. Her attitude was back. And she wasn't acting like she was half scared to ask him.

"There's not much else to tell. Coleman and I met in school or church, one or the other. It's been so long I can't remember. We've been good friends since, and that's pretty much it."

"I thought there was a girl?" Her voice was studiously innocent.

"You know, funny you should mention that." He picked up the cutting board, holding it in one hand while he put a hand on his walker and hopped to the stove.

"That's talent," she said, grinning at him.

"That's what I thought." He scraped the onions into the skillet while she stirred. "You're right. There was a girl. I guess I thought I was in love with her."

"You guess?"

"I thought. I did. I thought she was the one. Like capital THE ONE."

"Nice. But you found out she wasn't."

"Well, I believed for a long time that she was. I have a tendency to get stuck on things, and I just stay stuck."

He set the cutting board down on the counter, grabbing a rag and wiping it off.

"I thought it was a good characteristic. And I still think it is, mostly. You persevere. You are determined to make things work. You don't give up. You're not a quitter. You don't get sidetracked by the new things, the latest things, whatever everyone else is doing and awing over, you stick to what works. I don't know, maybe that's not an asset, but I thought it was."

"I think so. I mean, I think when you take anything to an extreme, it's going to be too much. The Bible talks about doing things in moderation."

"Yeah. So I guess when you take perseverance and determination to the extreme, you get stubbornness."

"Oh? Are we admitting to a vice?"

"A character flaw, more like it. Yeah. That'd be me."

"Wow. It wasn't hard to get you to admit it."

"No. I thought I was being faithful, I guess, but I think I was just in love with the memory. I thought she was better than what she was. Especially, looking back, it should have been a huge clue when she was dating me, and then cheated with someone else, and then left us both for someone else. I... I guess I just didn't want to admit that I was wrong. And I only saw the good in her, or maybe I just saw what I wanted to see. But at any rate, I wasn't interested in anyone else. I thought... I thought eventually she'd come back. And then, when it was pretty obvious that she wasn't going to, after five or so years, I guess I put her up on a pedestal in my mind, and no one else I met could measure up, if I even looked at them."

"So once you have your eyes on a girl, you don't look at any other girls? That's not a bad trait."

"It is when the girl that you're mooning over has totally forgotten about you, had children with someone else, and was living with her boyfriend when Dad and I went to look at a furnace they had advertised just a week ago."

"Wow!" She stopped stirring and turned to look at him. "You just saw her?"

"Yeah. Her name is Alana, and the image I had built up in my mind was a lot different than the reality."

"I see."

"Yeah. And Dad and I kind of talked about it, but if I'd been married to her, I would love her no matter what. But since I'm not, and I'm not tied to her in any way, she's not the kind of girl I want to have anything to do with."

"I see."

"She actually propositioned me on the porch, said she was looking to...trade up, I think she implied."

"That's a compliment."

He laughed. "I guess. But seeing her, she didn't really compare to..." He took a breath. "You."

The spatula stopped, and she held it suspended over the skillet. She didn't turn to look at him, and he felt like his heart stopped. He...thought it might be a good time to apologize, that maybe she believed him, but he hadn't meant to tell her how he felt before the apology had been accepted.

Too late for planning,

"You have some loose standards then," she said, not looking at him, and while her voice sounded teasing, there was a serious undertone that he hated.

She put her hand on the handle of the skillet, and he put his over top of hers.

"Wait. Please."

"I think I've heard enough," she said. "Thanks for telling me."

"Shasta."

He heard the way her name came out of his mouth, like a caress, like he was touching it gently, cherishing it, savoring it, and while he hadn't meant to, it was exactly the way he meant it. He'd say it again a thousand times like that, if she understood that that was the way he felt about her.

"Will you listen to me?"

"We already had this conversation. You know how I felt, and you were clear about how you felt. Do we really have to go through it again?"

"Do you mind talking to me instead of the skillet?"

A weak smile turned her lips up as she sighed and turned. Put out a little, and he didn't think she was faking it. She really didn't want to talk about this.

"I'm sorry. I'm sorry I said that. Even if... Even if it was true, if it was truly the way I felt. I... I was taken aback, and I didn't handle anything the way I should have."

"It's fine. You know my background. Foster kid. I'm tough."

She tried to turn away, but his hand tightened on hers.

"Please. Listen?"

She stopped, but her eyes were back on the skillet.

"The day after I said that to you is the day that Dad and I went and I saw Alana. I didn't want to say anything to you, because I didn't want you to think that I saw her and decided I didn't love her and decided to jump to the next nearest woman who was around. I... I guess you know that's not the way I am, and I hated that it seemed that way. It's just that seeing her made me realize that you had taken her place—I compared her to you and found her completely lacking. It made me realize what I had pushed aside because of my stubborn determination to stick to my childhood daydream. I also knew that a simple apology to you wasn't going to cut it. I figured that I hurt you pretty badly. Not because you said so, or because anyone said so," he hurried to go on, when she opened her mouth like she was going to deny it or tell him that she was tough again. "I just know how I would feel if you would have said that to me. It would have hurt. And I'm sorry. I'm sorry I hurt you. It... It's bothered me ever since, because that's the last thing I want to do. Is hurt you. I'd much rather see you happy and smiling."

One of her lips pulled back, maybe in irritation, or maybe because she wasn't buying what he was trying to sell her, and her head swung from the skillet to the counter and back to the skillet again, avoiding him.

"I was upset that night, because I hadn't expected to kiss you. But more than that, I hadn't expected to like it. Love it. Want to keep doing it. And then it was all I could think about. I wanted to hold you, kiss you, talk to you about all the things you wouldn't talk to me about, and I was jealous of the people that you did talk to. Jealousy isn't a fun emotion to feel."

"You weren't safe. I couldn't talk to you because you weren't safe."

He wasn't sure exactly what that meant.

His hand came up, and he took her chin and gently tugged so that her face was turned toward his. "What do you mean I wasn't safe?"

"I knew you didn't feel the same way about me that I felt about you. I knew I couldn't share my secrets with you, because you wouldn't care about them, be careful with them... I knew you wouldn't tell anyone. That's not the issue. It was that... I guess maybe being a foster kid, I learned to guard my thoughts and emotions. I couldn't let them out to just anyone. You never knew who might be telling on you, who might twist your words and get you kicked out, or moved, or get the entire school up in arms against you."

"Ouch."

"Ouch is right. But I moved pretty often, so I had the opportunity more than once to start again at a new school, and I learned even more to keep my mouth closed, to not share things. People don't care about your secrets. They don't care about your pain. They just care about themselves and...getting ahead."

"Not everyone."

"I know. That's why when I came to Sweet Water, when the whole town came together to help me, no one said a bad word, no one talked about anyone else, everyone just seemed to...love each other. I guess it feels too good to be true. Only you know, Sweet Water is real."

"There are bad apples in every bunch, but there are a lot of good people here."

"I know. And that's why it was so special to me and why I want to stay." She lifted her brows, as though asking him to understand.

And when she put it like that, he did. But they'd gotten away from everything he was trying to say.

"But I was talking about me. I can't believe you didn't trust me."

"It wasn't trust. I knew I could tell you things and you wouldn't blab them to everyone, it wasn't that. I knew, at least I was fairly sure, that you wouldn't laugh at me either. But I guess I just didn't think you cared. That what was important to me would be important to you, too. If I tell you my secrets, tell you those things I cared about, and you brush them off, forget, they wouldn't be important to you. And... I knew that would hurt me."

"I see," he said simply. And he realized that what she was saying right now were the secrets that she was talking about. The things she was afraid to trust him with because she didn't think he cared.

"So...you changed your mind about whether or not I care?"

"You caught that?"

"Sure did."

"It might be hard for you to believe, but when someone doesn't care about the things that you share with them, it makes you feel like they don't really care about you. When they don't remember the things you tell them, when they don't remember the things that are important to you. The things you share, and the things you show them. They can take it and treat it like a treasure, or they can take it and set it aside like it doesn't matter. I suppose, since I never really had too many material things, the things that came out of my heart became my treasure? And the way people treated those things when I took them and gave them carefully out told me how they felt about me."

Nolt just stood there in silence for a bit. She was so right. Maybe that was part of the reason why, when people got to know each other, they shared their past and their hopes and dreams, they shared secrets and achievements and excitement and sadness, and...they assumed that the other person was remembering the things they talked about, maybe not word for word, no one expected anyone to have a perfect memory, but to at least make the effort to tuck those things away, to show the person who shared them with them that they cared, that they considered the treasures of their heart valuable and they would put them somewhere safe.

"I've mentioned your age a couple times, and I'm ashamed of that as well. Not only because of what we talked about with you being more mature than most people your age, but with things like what you just said just now. I've never considered anything like that before, and while I guess I kind of knew it in my head, that when you care about someone, you pay attention to what they say, you remember it, you don't make them repeat themselves because you couldn't be bothered to pay attention and remember. But to say it the way you did, that just...makes total sense."

Maybe she had a shy smile hovering around her lips because of his sincere compliment.

He lifted his hand and ran it along her jawline, then wrapped it around her neck. "Were you paying attention when I said how much I thought about your kiss?"

"That felt like a hint," she said, looking up at him with her eyes smiling.

"Did it? Probably because it was."

"Oh yeah? So, if I ask you to kiss me right now, you'd say yes?"

"Maybe I'll just forgo the yes and get started right on the kissing."

"Maybe you want to ask me to move a little closer, because it's going to be a little awkward if you have to hop over here." She indicated the foot and a half or so that separated them.

"Maybe you could be a good nurse and walk to your patient so he doesn't have to hop around the kitchen and risk falling."

"Maybe you should strengthen those leg muscles and do a little of your physical therapy on your way over here."

She said that, but she walked forward, putting a hand on his waist, with her eyes on his face like she was watching to see if that was okay.

"I'm twelve years older than you are. Doesn't that bother you?" He had to ask. When he did the math in his head, he always sounded so much older than she was. It wasn't a little thing, because he would be considered old long before her. She was a young adult right now, while he was...flirting with middle age? Already middle-aged? He could hardly imagine that for himself, but it was true.

"It never has."

"What do you mean?"

"I guess, when we were talking about my college, I left out the fact that...every time Sadie talked about her brothers, I hung on her every word listening for anything about you."

His eyes flew over her face, looking to see her sincerity. She meant it. She really had had a crush on him for that long.

"And I never noticed you," he said, deflated. He couldn't believe she...stuck with him?

"What are you smiling at?" she asked.

"You know how I was telling you how I value perseverance and determination and faithfulness? Loyalty." He grunted. "That's you. Despite what I've done, despite me not noticing, despite me pretty much doing everything in my power, without even knowing it, to get you to stop crushing on me, you never did."

"No. It didn't matter how much you didn't notice me, or how much I heard Sadie talk about how you were pining over some girl that you loved in high school, or...even your rejection. I just decided that you got to choose who you liked, and I couldn't manipulate that."

"You didn't give up on me."

"You're worth it."

"I remember someone accused me of having low standards, maybe it's you whose standards should be a little higher."

"I have the highest standards. That's why I waited for you."

"So, if I told you that I wanted to be more than just friends, that I was thinking that courtship might be a good idea, you'd...be interested?"

She smiled, nodding her head.

"Think on that carefully, because I have a tendency to be very sticky, and once I get stuck, I'm kinda hard to remove."

"That's okay. Even though I'm young, I've found that I'm pretty sticky too."

"I think, I think we want the same things."

"Home? Kids? Roots?" she asked.

"Well, yeah, all that stuff too, but I thought we were both in agreement about the whole kissing thing too."

"Yeah. I kind of like the anticipation of thinking that I'm about to feel everything I felt the night of the auction, only, this time, I can be pretty sure that you're feeling the same thing too."

"Yeah, that might have been a good reminder. Maybe I should sit down. I was pretty dizzy after you were done with me that night, and being that I only have one good leg, I might end up on the floor."

"Well, as your nurse, I would highly recommend that you refrain from any activity that might make you dizzy."

"If I wanted to engage in activity that is almost certain to cause dizziness, could I convince you to engage in it with me?"

"How about we just stop talking about it and start doing it?"

He decided he didn't even need to answer that but lowered his head, pulling her close and kissing her the way he'd wanted to since the night of the auction

Epilogue

Six weeks later...

Nolt put his hand on the door to the basement and took a breath. It was never easy to eat crow, but he owed these ladies, and he would pay out.

"Changing your mind?" Shasta asked, with a lifted brow.

"No. Just, sometimes it takes a little fortification to face the ladies."

"They're not that scary."

"Maybe not to you. But I think they're a little rougher on me."

She rolled her eyes and shook her head, but she didn't disagree, and he figured she knew he was right. The ladies knew how to handle people, and Nolt figured sometimes men took a little bit of a rougher hand.

He could be stubborn.

He could admit that. Because it was true. But it was also true that Shasta didn't seem to mind. He looked again at the ring that sparkled on her finger. She had said yes.

"Nolt! And Shasta!" Miss Charlene said as they walked into the basement, closing the door behind him. Her blue hair waved softly as she looked them over, a smug grin on her face. "I don't like to gloat—"

"It's okay. You can gloat over this. Because I wanted to come and say you were right."

After he said that, Shasta held up her hand, showing off her ring and moving it around so it caught the light. The ladies squealed, grabbing their walkers and not exactly jumping up, but rising as quickly as they could from their workstations. He could almost hear the bones creaking.

They walked over, exclaiming over her ring, looking at how beautiful it looked on her finger, and Nolt had to agree. She was beautiful wearing his ring.

She looked beautiful in anything. Mostly because she looked at him and didn't see an old guy who was set in his ways, irritatingly insisting that he was right most of the time, commanding everyone around him, and more often than not bullheaded and stubborn.

Or maybe she saw those things and loved him anyway.

He liked to think that that was true. And from his experience with Shasta, it truly was. He only hoped he could love her in the same unselfish, selfless, giving kind of way. Where he'd give her anything she needed, and that included unconditional acceptance, as well as a solid foundation, a home with roots, and, God willing, children.

"So when is the big day?" Miss Teresa asked.

"I don't know, we haven't talked about that yet. I just said yes this morning."

"You asked in the morning?" Miss Kathy said, gasping.

"Everyone knows you're supposed to do it on an evening date, in candlelight, with violins or something playing." Miss Vicki shook her head sadly, like Nolt was a lost cause.

Maybe he was.

"He asked me with the sunrise in the background." Shasta's voice was dreamy, like he'd fulfilled all her wildest fantasies by proposing at some crazy hour in the morning.

But they'd been doing it together, watching the sunrise, and he knew how much she loved it.

"Oh. Well, if that's what you wanted."

"He did get down on one knee though, didn't he?" Miss Charlene insisted.

"That's why I waited until this morning. The cast just came off yesterday."

He'd wanted to propose to her for weeks now, but he wanted to do it on his knee. He wasn't sure why that was so important to him, maybe just letting her know that he wasn't afraid to kneel in front of her. It showed his deference and respect and showed her that she meant a lot to him.

At least, that's what it meant to him. He hadn't talked to her about what it might mean for her.

"Looks like you did all right," Miss Charlene said. Approvingly.

"Because of you. If you hadn't sent me to Shasta's house with that quilt, it probably wouldn't have happened. And I laughed at you, because I knew you were trying to set me up, and I was insisting that it wasn't going to happen. I wanted you to know I wasn't afraid to say I was wrong. Because I was wrong."

"That's okay. Sometimes we all just need a little push. And sometimes I'm happy to give one. That's what we do. If there weren't people in the world who needed pushes, we wouldn't have jobs."

"Well, you'd still quilt," Shasta said, looking at the material and the sewing machines and probably thinking about the quilt the ladies had made for her that she snuggled under every night.

"Oh, honey, that's just a cover. We're all about fixing people up and helping them get together with someone they can share the rest of their lives with." Miss Charlene waved a hand at Miss Teresa. "You can go ahead and write this one down in the books. We all called it."

"You keep records?" Nolt said, incredulously, and also feeling like that was probably something he would rather not know.

"Of course. We've only messed up once. It was big, and it really ruined our reputation, but we're working to reinstate ourselves."

"In sum, we're gonna try again on that one," Miss Vicki said, confidence in her tone. "It was meant to be, but sometimes things happen that are out of our control. We'll let it die down, then we're gonna give it another go. This time, it's gonna work."

"Some people just aren't meant to be together," Shasta said slowly.

But Nolt squeezed her hand. He remembered what his dad said, and he was pretty sure the ladies were talking about the same woman that his dad still thought about. There definitely was a chance for his dad and Mrs. Baldwin to end up together.

"I don't know, sometimes the strangest things happen, and two people who are extremely unlikely, and even maybe...enemies, might end up together."

The ladies and Shasta looked at him quizzically. He'd have to explain to her later.

For now, she just shook her head and turned back to Miss Charlene. "Since you guys are in the business of matchmaking people, do you take requests?" She looked hopefully at them.

"Go ahead and put yours in, although we're already working on our next couple. We got something set in motion, and this one is going to be epic." Miss Charlene actually rubbed her hands together.

Nolt coughed to cover his laugh.

The ladies might have called him out on it, but as soon as he was done, Shasta spoke again.

"My friend Sadie, Nolt's sister."

"Oh, honey, we know Sadie. We practically raised her from the cradle after her mom left. That crazy woman, she better not show her face back in Sweet Water again, there'd be a lynch mob after her, after what she did to those kids." Miss Charlene gave an apologetic glance in Nolt's direction. "Sorry about that, son, but she has it coming. The good Lord better take care of her."

"I'm sure He'll forgive her just as fast as He forgives anyone else. But to my knowledge, she's not sorry. If she's still alive."

Miss Charlene tsked and shook her head.

"Well, anyway, you know how sweet Sadie is, and she never really asks for anything for herself, but I know since she's been…old enough to notice, I guess, ten or twelve? Something like that. She's had a huge crush on someone, and I was wondering if maybe you ladies could do your little nudge thing, for Sadie."

"Of course. Who are you looking at?" Miss Teresa said, getting out a notepad and pen, like she was a reporter on the scene.

"You won't tell anyone?" Shasta said.

"Discretion is our trademark," Miss Charlene said with pride.

"Coleman Baldwin."

The ladies froze, and Nolt could tell right away that there was some kind of problem.

He looked around at them all. Miss Charlene shaking her head, Miss Teresa looking shocked, and Miss Vicki and Miss Kathy just looking guilty and sad.

"I'm afraid we can't do that," Miss Charlene said, waving a hand back at Miss Teresa. "We can't write that one down."

"Why not? Are they not compatible?"

"I don't know," Miss Charlene said, rubbing her chin a bit. "I'm not sure I buy into the whole soul mate thing. I mean, I think there are certain people that you are more compatible with than others, but I think as long as you're determined to make it work, it's more about shared values and a solid friendship."

She dropped her hand and looked a little sheepish. "I know I'm a matchmaker, but it's a complicated thing to try to figure out what's going to work, what's going to draw people together, what's going to set them apart and keep them from ever having any interest in someone. It's a delicate balance."

"So… Why can't you help Sadie and Coleman?"

"Because, honey. We already have Coleman set up to match with Peyton, the new single mom in town. I really think this is going to be—"

"Epic. I know. Do you think you could change the plan?"

Nolt's heart went out at the pleading in Shasta's voice and face. It hurt to see her want something so bad and not be able to get it, especially when it was something beautiful for someone else. For his sister. He'd not even known about that, and he was pretty sure Coleman didn't even know that Sadie was a girl. He wasn't even sure if he realized she was alive.

Considering that Nolt had been best friends with him forever, he would have heard about it if Coleman even had a thought in Sadie's direction.

"You never said anything," he said to Shasta.

"Sorry. I never swore not to tell, but that's the kind of thing that you know you just can't blab about."

He nodded.

"Tell you what," Miss Charlene said. "Once we have Peyton and Coleman together, then we'll find someone for Sadie."

Miss Charlene's words were comforting, but Nolt could tell they didn't appease Shasta. Still, there was nothing he could do. And maybe Sadie would be like him, stuck on a guy for so long until the perfect person came and opened her eyes.

The only difference was Sadie could see Coleman, and Nolt could say with confidence that Coleman was one of the few people he would trust with his little sister. He was an upright guy, honest and hardworking, and if he gave his word, he'd keep it.

Suddenly, a smile spread across Shasta's face. "You don't need a degree or anything to be a matchmaker. Maybe this can be a challenge? I'll try to match Sadie with Coleman, and you guys can match Coleman up with Peyton. We'll see which one works." She grinned a little bigger. "Teresa, you can write that down in your book."

Enjoy this preview of *Cowboy Rescuing Me,* just for you!

Cowboy Rescuing Me

Chapter 1

"Commitment."
- Barbara Harrison from Chestertown, MD

"We want you to help us match Coleman Baldwin with Peyton Sinclair, the new single mom who opened the bookstore and bake shop."

Sadie Powers stared at Charlene in shock. The basement of the church faded away, and her mind went blank before it revolted with a resounding "No!"

How could she do that? How could she try to get Peyton, who was new in Sweet Water but from what Sadie knew of her was a really sweet woman, to fall in love with Coleman?

It wasn't a matter of how, as in "what was she going to do in order to accomplish it." It was a matter of how, as in "this was something that would be impossible to work on because Sadie herself was in love with Coleman."

"Sadie? Are you thinking about it?" Charlene said, coming a little closer and putting her hand on Sadie's arm and peering into her eyes. "You seem to be friends with Peyton, and no matter how hard the other Piece Makers and I have tried, we just have not been able to get that woman to leave her bookstore, not for anything. She's...a total homebody."

"Which is what Coleman needs," Vicki said, still seated in her chair, piecing two quilt squares together.

"He does. He needs an anchor. Someone who can balance him and offset the other ladies in his family."

And there were a lot of ladies in his family. His dad had died over a decade ago, leaving Coleman as the sole man with five sisters and his mom, who had, with Coleman, taken over the business that her husband had left behind and turned it into the most successful auction barn in North Dakota.

She was strong and driven and successful and a little intimidating to Sadie.

"Someone quiet, who can provide a counterpoint to all the activity of the other ladies. Someone Coleman can lean on, who is strong enough to help him without losing her identity."

The other ladies nodded in agreement as Kathy spoke. She too was still sitting in her place, only she was sorting material.

"Basically, Peyton is absolutely perfect for Coleman, but we haven't been able to figure out how to get them together. Coleman hardly ever comes into town, and when he does, he's never stopped at the bookstore."

"She's starting to sell some baked goods there, since it used to be a restaurant before it closed down." Sadie tried not to make her words sound desperate. She really couldn't do what the ladies were asking.

"That won't last long. Sweet Water can't sustain two restaurants," Vicki said with assurance.

"That was back before Sweet Water had started growing. Now that we have so many new people and so many of the people who grew up here have been staying, maybe it can." Teresa, the last of the four ladies who were currently in the basement, looked serious as she stood at a table pulling batting out of a bag.

"You have a point. Maybe the baking will work," Charlene said, nodding thoughtfully.

"She's actually been making a recipe she said her mother passed down to her called berry French toast bake. She's been doing it on

Saturday mornings for the last month, and it's been popular, since she's sold out every week."

Sadie worked in the office at her family's trucking company. Fridays and Saturdays were long days, sometimes twelve or fourteen hours or more.

Since Peyton had opened the bookstore, she had tried to take time at some point on Saturday morning to stop in, originally to purchase a book to read for the week, but since Peyton had started with her berry French toast bake, the bookstore had smelled amazing, and Sadie couldn't pass up a chance to purchase a piece of it each time, too.

That must have been the way the rest of the patrons felt, and perhaps the scent had drifted out on the sidewalk and lured a few people in.

Regardless, the bookshop had started becoming rather busy on Saturday mornings. And Sadie had become friends with Peyton.

Could she watch her friend fall in love with the man she'd hoped would someday notice her?

She knew she could. If they were happy together, if they were meant to be, she could give up what she wanted and be happy for her friend. That's what friends did after all.

But she didn't want to. And Peyton wasn't interested in Coleman. At least, she could hardly be interested in someone she'd never met.

"I think you ladies are right. They just have completely different interests, and I don't even see them running into each other...maybe at church."

Even then, it seemed a little far-fetched. Coleman was friendly, but he didn't stick around and chat, since he had his own ranch to run in addition to the auction barn that he headed up for his family.

Sadie had never actually been out to his ranch. It wasn't something that could be seen from the road, and she'd never had a need to visit a single man living by himself who didn't realize she existed. Even though her brother Nolt was Coleman's best friend.

Coleman and Nolt were twelve years older than Sadie, and she'd always seemed like a baby to them, if they even thought of her at all.

"They have you in common," Charlene said decisively.

"Not really. I know that Coleman and Nolt are best friends, but it's not like Nolt still lives at home or that Coleman hangs out at the garage anymore. They both have their own lives, and when they do hang out, I'm not around."

"But you can suggest to Peyton that she send her son to Coleman to take riding lessons. Our sources have told us that Owen, who is twelve, loves horses. And Coleman has a few."

"But I don't know Coleman." Not really. Not enough to go to him and ask him to give riding lessons. "Not to mention, Peyton is on a very limited income, and I'm sure she can't pay for them."

"That's where you come in again," Charlene said, sounding proud of herself for coming up with this. "You can say something to Nolt, who can say something to Coleman about donating riding lessons to the single mom whose son loves horses but who can't afford riding lessons."

Sadie sighed silently, and her heart hung its head. That's exactly something Coleman would do. He was commanding and very businesslike, but he was always willing to lend a hand anywhere. And he would totally take a young boy under his wing with something like that. He might not set foot in the bookstore, but he was at home on the ranch, and he wouldn't have a problem helping a kid out. He'd always been very good with his younger sisters from what Sadie could see, although they were all older than she.

"It's brilliant, isn't it?" Vicki called from her seat across the room.

"I think it would work." Sadie tried to infuse some enthusiasm into her voice. To be excited and happy. Coleman was a great guy, and Peyton seemed like she truly was perfect for him, just like the ladies had said.

She was much closer to his age as well.

Although Sadie had never really considered her age a factor, she supposed it could be. Some people got hung up on things like that, but the ladies were right. Coleman probably wanted a mature woman. One who didn't engage with her brothers in creating elaborate practical jokes and enjoy rollerblading down Main Street at midnight and thought flying kites was a great way to spend a Saturday afternoon – a rare afternoon when she wasn't working.

No, the more she thought about it, the more she knew the ladies were right. She probably wouldn't be able to get over her crush on Coleman overnight, since she'd been nursing it for more than a decade, but maybe she just needed them to point out all the things that Coleman needed in a woman to know that they were all things that she really didn't have. She was too immature and fun-loving for someone like him.

"You're right. I'll help you, because Peyton is perfect for Coleman."

Pick up your copy of Cowboy Rescuing Me by Jessie Gussman today!

A Gift from Jessie

View this code through your smart phone camera to be taken to a page where you can download a FREE ebook when you sign up to get updates from Jessie Gussman! Find out why people say, "Jessie's is the only newsletter I open and read" and "You make my day brighter. Love, love, love reading your newsletters. I don't know where you find time to write books. You are so busy living life. A true blessing." and "I know from now on that I can't be drinking my morning coffee while reading your newsletter – I laughed so hard I sprayed it out all over the table!"

Made in the USA
Columbia, SC
17 May 2023

16875253R00096